Jed looked at  like a pretty happy kid to have just come from a grueling piano lesson.

"You know, I haven't heard you play for a long time. Want to play something for me? How about what you just played for your teacher?"

Mark glanced over at the piano, where his books were still sitting open to the correct page. "Sure."

Jed listened to him play. For an eight-year-old, the kid sounded good. As he recalled, Liz started him at the beginning of grade one, so he had been playing for nearly two years now. For a strict teacher, this Miss Jefferson must have what it took to put up with active kids like Mark. Mark obviously enjoying playing the piano, and he did well.

"So what's your teacher like?"

Mark opened his eyes wide. "Miss Jefferson? Her feelings get hurt if I don't practice, and she expects me to remember all the hard stuff. She makes me sit still, and both feet have to touch the floor." Mark paused to think. "And she's old."

GAIL SATTLER was born and raised in Winnipeg, Manitoba, and now lives in Vancouver, BC (where you don't have to shovel rain) with her husband, three sons, dog, and countless fish, many of whom have names. She began writing when the company she worked for closed and she chose to stay home with her children. She writes inspirational romance because she loves happily-ever-afters and believes God has a place in that happy ending. She now works part time as office manager for a web design company. Visit Gail's website at http://www.getset.com/gs

Books byGail Sattler

HEARTSONG PRESENTS
HP269—Walking the Dog

Don't miss out on any of our super romances. Write to us at the following address for information on our newest releases and club information.

Heartsong Presents Readers' Service
PO Box 719
Uhrichsville, OH 44683

Piano
Lessons

Gail Sattler

Heartsong Presents

Dedicated to the memory of my own piano teacher, Miss Isabel Kachinowsky, who made the music so much more than mere notes on the page.

All Scripture quotations, unless otherwise indicated, are taken from the HOLY BIBLE, NEW INTERNATIONAL VERSION®. NIV®. Copyright © 1973, 1978, 1984 by International Bible Society. Used by permission of Zondervan Publishing House. All rights reserved.

A note from the author:
I love to hear from my readers! You may correspond with me by writing: **Gail Sattler**
Author Relations
PO Box 719
Uhrichsville, OH 44683

ISBN 1-57748-481-9

PIANO LESSONS

© 1998 by Barbour Publishing, Inc. All rights reserved. Except for use in any review, the reproduction or utilization of this work in whole or in part in any form by any electronic, mechanical, or other means, now known or hereafter invented, is forbidden without the permission of the publisher, Heartsong Presents, PO Box 719, Uhrichsville, Ohio 44683.

All of the characters and events in this book are fictitious. Any resemblance to actual persons, living or dead, or to actual events is purely coincidental.

Cover illustration by Lauraine Bush.

PRINTED IN THE U.S.A.

one

Jed parked his truck but remained seated behind the wheel as he stared at the house. Back when they were teenagers, he and Liz had done nothing but fight. He'd been the worst kid brother imaginable, and he didn't know how it happened, but through phone calls and constant letters, it was almost unbelievable they had become so close as adults while living apart.

The kids' bikes lay strewn in the middle of the front yard, and squeals of laughter along with the dog's barking echoed from the back.

Suburbia. Happy family life.

Enter Uncle Jed.

Would he be a happy family addition, or an intrusion? Liz had invited him to stay, and after all, he would be earning his keep, but he wasn't sure he would like the big city of Vancouver. Even though Liz's house was in the suburbs, like his new job, it was too close to the city to suit him.

Leaving his belongings in the truck, he approached the house slowly. He would start his new job in a few days, but for now he felt like a poor, displaced relative.

He knocked and waited.

Liz answered the door with a huge smile, greeting him with a big bear hug before he had a chance to say a word.

"Jed! We've been so excited waiting for you. Come on in!" Liz turned to yell at the top of her lungs. "Mark, Betsy! Uncle Jed is here!"

Their screeches gained in volume until they rounded the

corner and pounced, almost knocking him down the stairs.

"Hey, ragamuffins! How's it going? And how's school? Got your diplomas yet?"

"Uncle Jed!" Betsy faced him with a scornful expression, her hands on her hips emphasizing her disdain. "They don't give dippalomanas out for kinnergarnernen."

Liz shook her head, scowled at Jed, then smiled at Betsy. "That's pronounced 'dip-lom-a,' and Uncle Jed will teach you to say it properly. And he can work on the word 'kinder-garten,' too."

Jed laughed. He loved to goad Betsy into using big words. "So, Mark, how's calculus?"

Mark scrunched his eyebrows, scowled in an expression that mirrored his mother's, and said nothing.

He ruffled Mark's already messy hair. "You mean they haven't got you doing calculus in grade three? What good is that school, anyway?"

"Uncle Jed!" Mark crossed his arms and tried to look angry, but his quivering grin gave him away. Jed mussed his hair even more.

Liz craned her neck over Jed's shoulder to see his truck. "Bring all your stuff?"

"Yup."

"In one load?"

Jed tried to give his shoulders a casual shrug and forced himself to smile. His 4X4 was big, but not that big—not that he had a lot of stuff left. "I sold everything big and put the rest away in storage. All I need is my clothes, bedroom furniture, and my stereo. I didn't think you wanted my couch and stuff in your family room."

"The sale go all right?"

"Yeah, I was lucky."

It had almost been too easy, but he could see God's hand at

work. After the plant closed, causing massive unemployment and a downturn in the local economy, he somehow had managed to find a buyer for his condo immediately, selling it for just enough to cover his outstanding mortgage. He'd also managed to find another job before his last penny ran out, albeit in the city. He moved as soon as the money came through. The only problem would have been finding a decent place he could afford to stay in only a short week before starting his new job, but Liz had taken care of that.

When her sitter quit only three weeks into the school year, Liz was desperate. Now that Betsy had started kindergarten, only the more costly day cares would provide transportation back and forth to the school—if she could even find an opening without being relegated to a waiting list.

Problem solved. Jed's new job on the evening shift would allow him to be home all day to baby-sit. Liz and Frank arrived home in plenty of time for Jed to drive the fifteen-minute trip and arrive on time for the second shift. All he had to do was start supper for the family, and of course keep up his share of the housework, and he had free rent and all his meals paid for until Betsy started full-day school next September.

The entire drive into town he had been lost in thought, both grateful and amazed everything had fit into place so smoothly and quickly. He dared not question why all his prayers had been answered, especially after he'd been so stupid.

Liz and Jed both started to speak at the same time. "I really appreciate. . ." They laughed in unison. Liz's eyes sparkled, lightening his spirit by one more notch.

"You first," he said.

Liz smiled up at him. "I was going to say, little brother, that I really appreciate you moving in to do this for me. I'm going to enjoy living with you again, because it's far cheaper to pay for your meals than to pay for day care." She cocked her head to one side. "Your turn."

Jed heaved a sigh of relief. He still worried about being an unwelcome guest or a financial burden, but Liz had again eased his fears. He wondered how she knew what he was thinking. Perhaps the reason they fought constantly when they were growing up was because they thought too much alike.

"I was going to tell you how much I appreciate you sharing your home and committing your family to putting up with me for a year. And don't count your chickens about the cost of keeping me. You haven't calculated the cost of my laundry." Jed pretended to have to pry his shirt off his chest, as if it were wet.

Liz hit his shoulder with a stuffed toy she had been carrying. "Frank will be home at 4:30, but if you want, we can start moving in the boxes and smaller things now."

As they walked out to the truck, Jed thought about Frank still at work. "So, why are you home? I thought you would be at work, and I was going to let myself in. I was really surprised to hear the kids at home." He jingled the contents of his pocket, fingering the shiny new key Liz had mailed him.

Liz sighed. "I couldn't find a sitter, so I had to take a few days off work until you got here, and they weren't very happy about it. If it's okay with you, I'd like to get back tomorrow. Are you ready to jump right in?"

He handed down a suitcase. "No problem. Just run down the routine for me. After all, what else do I have to do, except find a place for what little stuff I brought?"

As they walked back and forth together unloading the truck, Liz gave him the rundown on the daily routine. "Frank and I leave at 7:00. That means you have to get Mark up and get him ready. He has to be out the door for school at 8:20. Betsy usually wakes up when he leaves. Mark eats lunch at school, and Betsy has to be at school by 12:30. You'll have the afternoon to yourself, until you pick her up at 3:00. Mark gets off at 3:00 also, but he walks home with his friends. So if you can start supper, Frank and I get home at 4:15. Monday is soccer, Tuesday is Mark's piano lesson, Wednesday he may go over to a friend's house, Thursday is. . ."

"Whoa! I think I'm going to have to write all this down. How do you keep up? No wonder your sitter quit!"

Liz turned and stuck her tongue out at him. "You took the job, little brother."

Jed grinned at her. "I know." It was great to be home.

ঽ

Jillian checked her watch as she listened to little David pounding out each note of the song he was supposed to have practiced all week. She put on her best teacher's smile.

"David, I thought you said you practiced your piano lessons every day."

"I did. But I only played it once every day."

Jillian wanted to hit her head against the wall. If he practiced this song seven times over the past week, it surely would have sounded better than that. Instead she smiled at him again. "I'm going to have to ask you to repeat it for next week. I know you can do it with no mistakes. And don't forget to tap your foot. All the notes have to be on time with your foot. Okay, David?"

"Yes, Miss Jefferson."

"Your time is up now, and I see your mom's car in the front. Now, you practice it every day, and more than once." She closed the book and stood, prompting David to stand as well. "Good night, David."

"Good night, Miss Jefferson."

Jillian waved good-bye to the last student of the day. As she closed the door, her smile faded, and she immediately headed to the medicine cabinet to get something for her pounding headache.

Why did little David have to play so loud? It wouldn't be so bad if at least he got some of the notes right the first time. She wondered where his parents had the piano, and how they could stand it. It was almost as if he pounded every key as loud as possible on purpose, just to be annoying.

Her students ranged from kindergartners to high school students, beginners to advanced. By sheer coincidence, all her worst pupils were on Monday, and all her best ones were on Tuesday. She loved Tuesdays. But children grew up so quickly; soon they would all improve their skills or quit, and these days of headaches and frustration would be long forgotten. Once her schedule filled to capacity, she wouldn't be taking on so many beginners.

The best part of teaching piano lessons from her home was not having to fight traffic or worry about pleasing the boss. She only needed a few more students, and her appointment book would be as full as she wanted.

Sitting at the piano, she packed up the beginner lesson books, tidied up the pile of pass stickers and various other rewards for hard work, then selected a small pile of her own favorites. A Bach classic, her favorite Chopin collection, and a few praise books. After a day like today, she especially needed those. As she played, the music soothed her shattered nerves, and her mind drifted ahead to the next day's schedule.

On Tuesday, the best day of the week, she most appreciated her lesson with Mark Edwards. Even at eight years old, Mark demonstrated real talent, along with a desire to excel. Eager, intelligent, he had a real love for music. If only all her students could be more like Mark.

❧

Jed held Betsy in his arms, and they waved to Liz and Frank

as the car backed out of the driveway. It had been 3:30 in the morning before he had his stuff organized enough to go to bed. Now, only three and a half hours later, Betsy was up for the day.

"Uncle Jed?"

Jed answered and yawned at the same time. "Yeah, Pumpkin?"

"Are you really going to live with us until I get to stay in school all day?"

"You bet."

"Are you going to like living with us?"

"Sure." He yawned again.

"Can you help me ride my bike?"

"Yup."

"And play baseball like Mark?"

"Yeah, sure."

"I can print my name. My teacher says I'm doing real good. Can you help me print my phone number?"

"Yeah, sure."

"With a pen?"

"Yeah, with a pen."

"And when will you teach me to tie my shoes?"

Why was the kid asking these hard questions? Didn't she know what time it was? "Tomorrow." Jed lowered her feet to the floor. Was she always such a yacky little thing so early in the morning? Liz had told him Betsy didn't get up until much later.

The alarm on his wristwatch beeped as Jed stifled another yawn, signaling time to get Mark up for school. "Tell you what. I'll give you a nickel if you go wake your brother up for me." He remembered Liz waking him up for school one morning by pouring water on his head. Betsy was too young for that, for now. Maybe one day. . .

"Mark! Mark!"

Jed flinched at the volume of Betsy's voice as she screamed loud enough to wake the dead, never mind an eight-year-old boy.

"Shut up!"

"Wake up! Uncle Jed said so!"

"Shut up!"

"Uncle Jed! Mark told me to shut up!"

"Did not!"

"Did too!"

"Shut up!"

"Uncle Jed! He did it again!"

What had he done? What had he gotten himself into? How long would it take to pack up all his stuff again? Jed slumped, sitting heavily on the couch. He waited for Betsy to run into the kitchen and Mark to shuffle along before he started to push himself up to follow.

A bang sounded from the kitchen, followed by a huge thud, then a crinkling sound.

"Uncle Jed! Mark spilled the cereal!"

"Shut up, you fink!"

"Uncle Jed! Mark told me to shut up!"

"Knock it off!"

"And he's calling me names!"

Jed groaned. "I'll be right there."

As Jed entered the kitchen, he observed Mark furiously scooping the cereal off the floor and shoveling it back into the box with his hands, while behind him the dog licked it off the floor, eating as fast as she could.

Surrounded by a ring of cereal on the floor, Betsy jumped up and down, shrieking, and grinding it into small crumbs, sending bits and pieces all the way across the room. "Uncle Jed! Uncle Jed!" she cried out, waving her arms in the air.

Jed closed his eyes. What now? If he could find something else to feed them, he would clean up later. He wondered if Liz had another box of cereal hidden somewhere. With a little imagination and determination, Jed found some bowls and a box of instant oatmeal. Carefully reading the directions, he plugged the kettle in to boil, and waited.

According to the clock on the wall, they were fast running out of time. Jed measured and poured the water, turned his face back to the table, and opened his mouth to speak, but Mark was gone.

Mark's voice drifted from the living room. "Uncle Jed, I think the dog was sick."

Jed checked the clock. Now they were really running out of time. "What? Where?"

"In front of the TV, on the rug."

Not now. Why was this all happening? Was cereal bad for dogs? If so, how come the kids could eat it with no ill effects? He grabbed the roll of paper towels and strode into the living room, where an ugly blob lay on the rug in front of the television. Jed's stomach flipped over. Good thing he hadn't eaten yet, or he would have been next, right along with the dog.

Mark stood to the side, his hands covering his mouth and his shoulders shaking. Jed tried to keep from puking himself as he looked down at the mess. As Mark started to laugh out loud, Jed became more suspicious.

"Mark!" he shouted. "This is plastic! I'll get you!" He started to chase after Mark, feeling bits of dry cereal crunching under his bare feet as he ran, but Mark managed to keep one step ahead of him. Mark dashed into the bathroom and locked the door, howling with laughter the whole time.

Betsy stood on the coffee table, pointing at the closed bathroom door. "I'm telling Mom! You're gonna get it!"

Jed sucked in a deep breath. He was never having kids.

Never. "Come on, Mark, it's time to eat and get ready for school."

Mark opened the door a crack and peeked out.

Jed ran one hand down his face as he squeezed his eyes shut. "Come on, Mark. Just get ready for school."

Without a word, Mark shuffled into the kitchen. By now the oatmeal was cold, and both of them ate only a couple of small spoonfuls, complaining bitterly the entire time. Jed sagged in his chair while they argued over who got to look at the brightly colored box.

As Jed watched, he had a nagging impression that there was something he should have been doing, but for the life of him he couldn't remember what it was. Mark pushed the bowl of cold oatmeal to the center of the table with a loud scraping sound, then returned to his bedroom to get dressed. Jed checked the time again, worried that Mark was going to be late if he didn't move a little faster.

"Come on, Mark, move it!" he called out, trying to keep the irritation out of his voice.

Running out of his room, Mark turned to the front door.

"Did you brush your teeth and comb your hair?"

"Oops." Mark ran into the bathroom, and came out in record time. Jed wondered if the toothbrush was even wet, but didn't push it.

Mark grabbed his backpack from the kitchen floor and stopped dead. "Uncle Jed? Where's my lunch?"

Jed leaned his head back and slapped his palm to his forehead. He knew there was something he was supposed to have done.

As quickly as he could, he dug through the fridge and found the sandwich Liz had made, then threw in an apple and a couple of cookies. He found a thermos in the cupboard with a picture of some superhero on it, filled it with milk, and rammed it into Mark's backpack.

"I'm going to be late now. You have to drive me."

"What? I'm still in my pajamas!"

"I'm going to be late."

"What about Betsy?"

"You have to bring her."

"She's still in her pajamas!"

"But Uncle Jed! I'm going to be late! You're going to make me get lines!"

Jed stared at Mark with his mouth hanging open, on the verge of telling Mark it was his own fault, but he stopped. Lines. He would never live it down, especially on his first day taking care of them. Jed ran into his room and quickly tossed on the first thing he touched. He bundled Betsy's coat over the top of her pajamas and slipped her sneakers over her bare feet.

"Let's go. We can still make it."

He hustled the kids into his truck and arrived at the school as the bell rang. Mark leaped out of the truck and ran into the school yard, and Jed turned around and drove back to the house.

"Well, Pumpkin, we made it." He pulled into the driveway. "What do we do now?"

"You forgot to let Missy out."

Was this a problem? "So?"

Betsy's big brown eyes opened wide at him, reminding him of a chubby-cheeked chipmunk. "I hope she didn't go peepee on the rug."

That was all he needed. This time it wouldn't be fake. He hurried with the key, listening to the dog barking furiously from the other side of the door. As he opened it wide, Missy ran into the front yard to relieve herself. At least one thing had gone right this morning.

Maybe he had bitten off more than he could chew.

Coffee. He needed coffee. Bad. Maybe ten coffees.

"Uncle Jed?"

He clenched his teeth, then forced himself to relax as he looked down at Betsy. If he heard one more "Uncle Jed" he was going to scream. "Yeah, Pumpkin?"

"Can I watch TV?"

"You bet."

In silence, Jed hung up Betsy's coat, slid her sneakers by the door, and settled Betsy in front of the television. He started a pot of coffee and sat down, elbows resting on the table, his chin cupped in his palms, and watched it drip. The heady aroma of coffee soon filled the room. Had it really only been an hour since he had been dragged out of bed?

❧

Jillian smiled, inhaling the fresh morning air as she opened the window wide. Tuesday, her favorite day. Her smile widened at the thought of her first lesson later that afternoon. Mark Edwards, her favorite student.

The hardest part of teaching piano lessons for a living was finding things to keep her busy all day, and then as soon as school was over, working nonstop, often not taking the time for supper until lessons ended at 8:00. She paid the price for working such short hours on the weekends, however, which were filled with lessons from early morning till midevening. Many Sundays she spent time after church with students who needed extra help, especially at exam time, but it was worth it. She managed to earn a living from her home, even if it did mean seldom keeping company with other adults. In many respects, she welcomed the chance to keep to herself. No one asked her out anymore, and she liked it that way.

Jillian sighed. After running a few errands today, she had tentative plans to visit her sister. Except for Sue's screaming children, she enjoyed those visits. It also made her appreciate the calm, well-behaved kids she taught.

As the day wore on, despite the best of intentions, Jillian ran out of time, arriving back at home with barely enough time to get a pot of coffee started before her first student knocked at the door.

"Hello, Mark," she greeted him cheerfully as she sat in her chair beside the piano. "How is that new piece coming?"

"I really like it, Miss Jefferson, and I think I'm doing okay, except I don't have my book again. Can I borrow yours?"

Jillian picked through her pile of extra books. "Did the sitter forget to pack it again? I think maybe you're going to have to try harder and remember to pack your books yourself from now on."

Mark grinned. "No, the sitter quit. My uncle is staying at our house to look after us. I guess he forgot. He had a bad morning. I thought he was gonna, you know, like, hurl, when he saw what Thomas lent me."

Jillian didn't even pretend to understand as she opened her spare Level Three book to the correct page. "Well, let's get started. Can you do it hands together?"

She watched him work the selection with amazing ease, especially for the first week on a new and difficult number.

They discussed what needed improvement, and Jillian carefully complimented him on what he did well. After reviewing a couple of songs from past weeks, the lesson progressed quickly, and they soon ran out of time.

Her next student waited patiently, sitting in the chair next to the door. Jillian dismissed Mark and called Ashley up to the piano.

❧

"Uncle Jed!" Mark called as he walked in the door.

Jed cringed. "Yes, Mark."

"You forgot my piano books. Miss Jefferson is mad at you. She said I have to pack my music books myself now."

"Is that so?"

"Yeah, she's real strict."

Jed looked at Mark's smiling face. He looked like a pretty happy kid to have just come from a grueling piano lesson. "You know, I haven't heard you play for a long time. Want to play something for me? How about what you just played for your teacher?"

Mark glanced over at the piano, where his books were still sitting open to the correct page. "Sure."

Jed listened to him play. For an eight-year-old, the kid sounded good. As he recalled, Liz started him at the beginning of grade one, so he had been playing for nearly two years now. For a strict teacher, this Miss Jefferson must have what it took to put up with active kids like Mark. Mark obviously enjoying playing the piano, and he did well.

"So what's your teacher like?"

Mark opened his eyes wide. "Miss Jefferson? Her feelings get hurt if I don't practice, and she expects me to remember all the hard stuff. She makes me sit still, and both feet have to touch the floor." Mark paused to think. "And she's old."

two

After a few weeks of baby-sitting, Jed was ready to climb the walls. Mark and Betsy got away with all that nonsense the first day, but since then, their behavior had greatly improved. He had been tested, he put his foot down, and that was the end of it.

With the family all settled into their new routines after the flurry of the beginning of the school year, Jed managed to get Mark off to school with no more shenanigans, entertain Betsy all morning, feed her lunch, and take her to school with no difficulty. During his solitary afternoons, after his daily devotions and Bible reading, he discovered there were only so many times he could wipe the same counter. All he did was walk from room to room, when he wasn't pacing. And it gave him too much time to think.

The new job was going to work out, but his assigned menial duties didn't help his frustration level one bit. The other men were companionable enough, but they lacked any spark or vision for the future. Stuck in a dead-end job, not a single one of them seemed to mind. At least for him, the job was only temporary until next September, when he would enter college, provided he could get back on his feet. He would do anything to see that it happened, and this time nothing would stop him.

Jed mentally kicked himself for being such a pushover as he straightened the towels in the bathroom, then stood back to admire Liz's decorating scheme. One day he'd have a house like this. Never again would he let anyone take advantage of him as he had in the past.

He stood in silence in the empty house, wondering what he should do next. The guys had invited him for a beer before work, the same as they did most days, but Jed turned them down. Not only did he consider it a bad idea to drink before work, he just plain-old didn't drink. He didn't want to be labeled a religious fanatic, but as a Christian, his decision had been made. At twenty-six, he definitely was no angel, but he did his best to live his life according to God's direction.

Working the afternoon shift effectively put an end to any potential social life. Aside from the fact that he didn't know anyone in this city except for his sister and her husband, the only church activity during the daytime was the ladies' Tuesday morning Bible study and coffee time. He simply wasn't that desperate. Yet.

Jed picked up a few Lego pieces and tossed them into the box in Mark's bedroom, then paused for a split second, actually considering dumping the box and building something. Jed shook his head, almost screaming in frustration. Surely he was going around the bend. All alone with nothing to do. All day. Every day. He'd never considered himself a social butterfly, but he always found it easy to meet people. He liked the activity and atmosphere of a large busy church, where there was always something going on, but working the evening shift put an end to his participation. Give it a couple more days, and he was going to welcome the opportunity to dust the top of the door frames. With Liz's meticulous housekeeping, he couldn't finish up anything except for what they had previously agreed upon, and that wasn't much.

In the solitude of the empty house, as he passed the lonely piano, Jed tried to plunk out a melody with one finger. Before he left for work, Jed often listened to Mark practice his piano lessons. Mark had shown him a few notes, but Jed felt too awkward to ask the kid to teach him a tune.

As he passed the piano again, Jed tried to plunk out a melody with one finger. As a boy, he had wanted to learn to play the piano, but his parents didn't have the money or a piano. Now that he was alone, no one could listen or watch him make a fool of himself.

He dug through the drawer in the kitchen and found Liz's address book. Flipping the pages one at a time, he finally found what he was looking for under "P." Piano teacher, Miss J. Jefferson. Jed dialed the number.

 ❧

Jillian heard the phone ringing as she fumbled with her grocery bags and the bulky key ring. She deposited her groceries on the floor and picked up the cordless phone beside the piano, but it was dead. Not wanting to miss the call, she ran up the stairs to answer before it stopped.

"Hello?" she answered breathily, trying not to sound like she was panting.

"Is this Miss Jefferson, the piano teacher?" a male voice asked.

"Yes, speaking. Can I help you?"

"Do you have any openings?"

Her heart beat faster. Another student! She prayed he was going to ask for a day that still had a space available. Jillian held her breath for a second to try to steady her voice. "Yes, I do. What day would be best?"

The caller paused, as if thinking. "Doesn't matter. Every day's the same to me. How about tomorrow?"

She knew the answer without checking her schedule. "Yes, I have an opening tomorrow. How does 4:45 sound?"

"Too late. Let's see. I've got to work around kindergarten hours, so somewhere around 2:15?"

Jillian shuddered at the thought of taking on another five-year-old. The kindergarten kids had such a short attention span, and at the beginning of November, most of them hadn't learned enough of their alphabet to know what notes they were playing. Their legs were too short for their feet to touch the floor, and they wiggled the entire lesson. Often, after being in kindergarten all morning, by midafternoon they were too tired to concentrate.

Did she have the energy for this? Jillian fumbled to dig a pen and a scrap of paper out of her purse, which was still slung over her shoulder. "Yes, that would be fine. And the name?"

"Jed Davies," the deep voice of the caller announced.

She hesitated before writing it down. A few kids that age had already had lessons, and were getting pretty good. She tried to convince herself that it was entirely possible that this would be one of them. Hopefully he knew enough of his alphabet so she wouldn't have to waste the first lesson on simple ABC's.

Jillian shrugged her shoulders as she scribbled with the pen, trying to convince it to write. It was unusual for the father to be calling to enroll a child for lessons. She smiled to herself as the pen finally began to write, thinking how nice it would be if more fathers showed a little enthusiasm for their children's musical education.

Jed listened to the scratching noises, wondering if old Miss Jefferson was writing an entire novel, rather than just his short name.

"Fine, Mr. Davies. And do you have a book?"

Silence hung over the line, until Jed realized that by saying "Mr. Davies," Miss Jefferson was speaking to him. He hadn't thought about a book. Liz probably wouldn't mind if he borrowed Mark's old book. In fact, she would probably laugh. "Yes, I've got one."

"Good. I'll see you tomorrow at 2:15. Thank you for calling."

Jed hung up the phone. Old Miss Jefferson had been a little

out of breath when she answered the phone. He tried to picture the little old lady who would be teaching him piano lessons. Jed laughed out loud as he tucked the phone book back into the drawer. Wait until he told Mark and Liz this one.

As he glanced at the clock, he welcomed the time to go pick up Betsy from kindergarten since, except for work, this was his only opportunity to talk to other adults.

Jillian retrieved her spilled groceries, then prepared to psyche herself up for her Monday lessons. Someday some of these kids might be good. Someday they might remember their piano teacher with fond memories. Someday their feet would touch the floor.

ಌ

Jed approached Miss Jefferson's house carrying Mark's old book under his arm. Mark made him drive by yesterday on the way to soccer practice just so he could show off his teacher's house. Jed sucked in a deep breath and knocked.

A young woman about the same age as himself or maybe a bit younger answered the door. Her wavy, shoulder length auburn hair framed a perfect oval face. Wide, gorgeous green eyes stared up at him. He thought the woman could have been on a makeup commercial, only she wasn't wearing any. Her figure was model perfect, but she was too short to be a model, probably only about five-foot-five or so.

His mind wandered back to his conversation with Mark. This woman had to be old Miss Jefferson's daughter. But Mark had said "Miss" Jefferson. Was she a niece or something? He didn't know what to say, or who to ask for, Miss or Mrs. Jefferson, or her mother. Or her aunt?

His brain froze as she stared at him, expecting him to say something. He tried to shut out the impulse to get to know her better. He wasn't interested in available women. He was here for piano lessons.

"Can I help you?" she asked.

Jed swallowed and shuffled the book from one hand to the other. "I'm here to see Miss Jefferson."

Jillian blinked to stop herself from staring. When she opened the door for her newest student, the sight of the boy's father had rendered her speechless.

Mr. Davies was breathtakingly handsome. And tall. And not what she had anticipated. A fabulous mane of wavy light brown hair framed his strong dark features, and snug-fitting jeans showed off strong muscular legs.

And he was rather young-looking for the father of a five-year-old, but it was possible. She estimated his age at about the same as her own or maybe a bit older, probably about twenty-five. And where was the child? "I'm Miss Jefferson."

Jed opened his mouth, but no words came out. He swallowed again, hating himself for being so suddenly tongue-tied. "You're Miss Jefferson?" he blurted out. His gaze traveled up and down her one more time, before he fixed his eyes to her face. "I was expecting someone, um, older. Um, I mean, uh, your hair is brown, uh. . ." Actually, he didn't know what he meant! Jed's cheeks grew warm, and he was sure his ears were beet red as well. On top of it, he was stammering like an idiot. Mark had told him the piano teacher was old. Was the kid blind? But then again, Mark thought kissing girls was disgusting.

Miss Jefferson's eyes widened, showing off a deep sea green that nearly took what was left of his breath away. She inhaled sharply, then turned her head, searching for something behind him. "Where is little Jed?" she asked.

The corners of Jed's mouth quivered. He was six-foot-one. "I've been called many things in my life, but 'little' was never one of them. I'm Jed." He smiled down at her, extended one hand, and waited.

Jillian tilted her head back to let her gaze travel up to his face at the same time as she lightly touched his hand, giving him the limpest handshake of her life. Although she wondered why he had blushed when she introduced herself, now the heat crept up her face as well. She retracted her hand abruptly.

"Oh," she mumbled. As she made eye contact, his quirky little smile nearly made her knees give out. "You're an adult." She cringed inwardly at her brilliant observation. "I was expecting someone, um. . .someone younger. You were asking about kindergarten hours." Jillian mentally kicked herself. At first she thought his stammering was cute. Now she was doing no better.

"My niece is in kindergarten, so I need to do lessons when she's in school."

Jillian blinked twice in rapid succession. Niece? "The lessons are for you?" She kept staring, lost in the deep blue of his eyes until a wisp of her hair blew into her face, drawing her attention to the fact that they were still standing in the open doorway. "Oh, I'm so sorry, please come in."

She led him to the piano and motioned for him to sit beside her on the bench. "I don't have any adult students. Please excuse me, I'm afraid you caught me off guard. Shall we start?" She smoothed her sleeves in an effort to compose herself.

The bench creaked with his weight as he sat. They both looked at each other, stood, then Jillian pulled the bench further back to accommodate the length of his legs, and they sat down again.

Jillian concentrated on the obviously used lesson book that her new student placed on the piano. "Can you read music?" she asked, wondering if he had taken lessons as a child and given up.

He shook his head. "No. I'm a beginner. Mark showed me where middle C is. That's all I know." He plunked out middle C with his index finger.

"Mark?"

Jed nodded, turned his head, and smiled at her. "Yeah, Mark Edwards. He's my nephew. Plays well, doesn't he? He's the one that gave me your name. He thinks this is real funny, that I'm going to take piano lessons from his teacher."

Jillian tried to collect her befuddled brain as her newest student flashed a dazzling white smile at her. Mark Edwards? This was the uncle who didn't pack his music book last week? The one who was staying with them because the sitter quit? Her voice came out in a croak. "Yes, he is one of my better students."

He continued to smile at her, and Jillian fought to keep from becoming undone. She turned her body to the piano and focused on the keyboard. "Well," she mumbled, "let's get started." She played some notes on the piano, asking him to name them, then asked a few questions to see what he knew so far.

Next, she placed his hands on the keyboard and showed him the proper hand position, curving his fingers and placing them individually on the keys. He had wonderful hands for a man. His skin was soft, and she admired the little bit of hair showing from under the cuffs of his shirt. She tried to stop herself from blushing at noticing such a thing.

"Now, Mr. Davies, you must maintain proper posture. Keep your back straight, no slouching. Elbows in, feet flat on the floor at all times."

He laughed at her seriousness. "Please, call me Jed. I'm not old enough for anyone to call me Mr. Davies. And I can see what Mark meant about you being strict. He isn't very happy about you making him sit still and keep his feet on the ground."

Jillian tried to smile back. "I guess you should call me Jillian. I'd feel silly if you called me Miss Jefferson like the kids do. And Mark does very well sitting still and maintaining his posture when he is playing. He is very well-behaved."

Well-behaved? Jed remembered the plastic dog vomit and the subsequent chase around the living room on his first morning at the house. It would be years before he forgot that one.

He sat still as Jillian opened the book and showed him the first few songs, all of which required only one hand, four songs in all. Before he knew it, the lesson was over.

"This is it?" he asked.

"That's half an hour. Actually, we covered much more than I usually do in one lesson. Now you have to practice for a week, and come back and play these songs perfect for me."

Jed couldn't believe it. Was that all there was to playing piano? "If this is all I get to do, can I have another lesson when I'm done, even if it's not a week? I've got nothing else to do all day."

Jillian faced him. It was true, the first lessons were very simplified, but this series was a good progressive course. She wished he had brought a book more suited for adults. "Well, I don't generally. . .but I suppose I could make an exception. When you're ready, call in the morning and we'll see if we can set something up."

Jed checked his watch, noticing that it was time to go to the school to pick up Betsy. "Great." He stood. "I'll do that."

Jillian's heart beat far too fast as she escorted him to the door and watched him leave, taking long lazy strides as he walked. To say this was not what she expected would be a massive understatement. As hard as she had tried to concentrate, she'd found herself being distracted by his closeness as she tried to teach him the basics. Her face flushed as she remembered calling him Little Jed. Little Jed, indeed!

Jed walked quickly once he rounded the corner on his way

to the school. He didn't know why he'd tried so hard to look casual as he left Jillian standing on her doorstep, but he could feel her watching him as he walked down the street. He just knew.

How in the world was he going to learn anything with a teacher like that? Throughout the entire lesson, he'd found it difficult to concentrate on the lesson, hypnotized by her sweet melodic voice and gentle manners. He'd forced himself to listen to what she was saying, rather than how she was saying it.

His lips tightened and his pace became more determined. He could not allow this distraction. If he ever got the urge to get back into the dating scene, Liz said she knew a number of nice single women at her church whom she wanted to introduce to him. When he was ready, that would be the route he would take. Later. Much later. Like when he graduated from college. And got a good job teaching in a big high school. And then, only after many years. Maybe when he became the department head. Or principal.

If he could get past Jillian's annoying sweetness, piano lessons were going to be fun. And he was going to have to speak to Mark about his definition of "old."

He arrived at the school with perfect timing to take Betsy home.

❧

Mark raced out the school door and straight to Miss Jefferson's house. He had remembered to put his music books in his backpack all by himself this morning.

His teacher was waiting for him.

"Hi, Miss Jefferson!" he called as he walked up to the piano, throwing his backpack on the floor beside the bench. "Was Uncle Jed here today? He said he was going to take piano lessons. He's going to use all my old books." He gazed up expectantly at her, but Miss Jefferson only smiled politely at him and nodded. "Yes, Mark. He was here." She patted the bench and smiled again, so it didn't look like she was going to thank him for showing Uncle Jed all the notes. "And did you practice those hard ones this week?"

Mark didn't want to pout like his little sister. "Yes," he mumbled. "I had to practice lots to show Uncle Jed how much fun it was to play piano. He kept asking me to play stuff for him."

"Oh, really? Was he impressed? Did you do your best?"

Mark nodded so fast his hair fell into his eyes. "Yes, I practiced real hard." He sat straight and tall, both feet on the floor, and played his best for Miss Jefferson, showing her how well he had played for uncle Jed.

Jillian was impressed as she watched Mark play. It seemed having his uncle take lessons was going to be good for Mark. However, the unsettled feeling his Uncle Jed had left might not be so good for her.

"Very good, Mark, you passed them all! I can tell you worked very hard." She placed a large colorful sticker on each of the pages as he grinned excitedly. "Now, let's start the next page. I think it's going to be a fun one."

Jillian continued on with Mark's lesson, and tried to put thoughts of his uncle Jed aside. Would he really call before next Tuesday? Against her better judgment, she hoped he would.

She sent Mark on his way on time and welcomed her next student.

★

Jed heard the door slam over the sound of running water as he washed the potatoes he was preparing for supper.

Mark's loud voice almost caused him to drop the knife. "Uncle Jed! Uncle Jed!"

"I'm in the kitchen!" Jed shouted back. "What do you want? I have to get ready for work."

"Uncle Jed! I passed them both!"

Jed wiped his hands so he could admire the new stickers in Mark's book. Would he get stickers for passing? He hoped not. What would she do when he passed?

The sound of a car pulling into the driveway made him rein in his thoughts. If that was Liz and Frank getting home, that left him ten minutes to make it out the door to be on time for work.

Jed turned the heat down on the potatoes and gave the roast a poke with a fork to check its progress. Roast beef sandwiches for lunch tomorrow.

Packing his lunch pail, Jed wondered if this was a good time to get some information out of Mark, who was sitting at the table admiring his new stickers.

"So, Mark," Jed said as he casually searched the fridge for the bag of apples, "Miss Jefferson seems like she's a good teacher. She's pretty too. But she really isn't that old."

"But, Uncle Jed! Look at her! She has to be almost as old as Mom. I'll bet she's as old as you."

Jed straightened his back and cleared his throat. He swiped his hair back, then patted the top of his head, just to make sure there weren't any thin spots he didn't know about. As far as he knew, there were no gray ones either.

When Mark stared up at him with a stunned expression, Jed couldn't take it anymore. "Get out of here!" He stepped forward, pretending to chase Mark, lunch pail in hand. Mark squealed, prompting Jed to give chase for real, until he almost collided with Liz and Frank in the hall.

"Hi, Jed." Liz flattened herself against the wall as Jed skidded to a halt. "So, how was your piano lesson? You did go today, didn't you? And what did you think of Miss Jefferson?" He watched Liz bite back a grin. "She certainly has a way with children."

Jed narrowed his eyes to stare at his sister. "I'm leaving," he mumbled, just loud enough for her to hear.

She pointedly ignored him as she peeked into the oven. "Have a nice night at work then. See you."

"Yeah. Save some for me, will ya?"

"Bye, Jed," Frank said absently as he walked past Jed and opened the lid of one of the pots on the stove. "What's for supper?"

Jed didn't answer.

As he drove to work, Jed anticipated the next afternoon. After he dropped Betsy off at the school, he could start practicing his piano lessons.

&

Friday finally came. Not that the beginning of the weekend made much difference, since Jillian scheduled a full day of lessons Saturday, making it her busiest day.

She had just switched on the coffeemaker when the phone rang.

"Hi, Jillian? It's little Jed."

Jillian's face flushed, and she was relieved he couldn't see her. She had a feeling she would never be able to forget calling him that. "Yes, Jed?"

"Got time for a lesson today? I'm getting bored with these four one-handed tunes."

Obviously he had no clue that every afternoon was open. "Yes, today would be fine. Same time?"

"Yeah, sure. See you later. Bye."

Jillian dressed in her oldest jeans and rattiest T-shirt, deciding to keep to her original plan of scrubbing out her window frames, a job she had been putting aside for months. While she was in the process of dumping the dirty water down the drain, the doorbell rang. She cringed as she looked at the clock. If it was Jed, then he was early, and she was wearing her grubbiest clothes. But no matter. She couldn't leave him standing outside just because she wasn't ready.

Jillian answered the door with her heart in her throat. So much for her dignified professional image. "Hi, Jed. Come in. I'm afraid I lost track of the time, and I'm not ready."

He stood at the door, also dressed in jeans, but he wore a neatly pressed cotton shirt instead of a stained old T-shirt, and he, at least, was clean. He shrugged his shoulders. "Sorry. I think I'm a bit early."

"Well, come in." She couldn't very well leave him in the living room while she ran off to change. They would have to do the lesson as she was.

Instead of sitting beside her on the piano bench, Jed stood to the side, gripping his book with both hands. She followed his gaze, first to her accumulation of music books on her bookshelf, then to the praise book she had left open on the piano. She usually felt awkward about people seeing her church music, but thankfully Jed didn't say anything.

"Can you play something for me?" he asked, catching her off guard.

Jillian bit her bottom lip. "I guess so," she replied. "Anything in particular you'd like to hear?"

"Well," he drawled as he continued to study the pile of books, "how about something I could expect to be able to play a few years down the road?"

Jillian didn't want to hurt his feelings, but she hadn't a clue what level he could expect to be at. She had no idea if he had any real talent; after all, this was only his second lesson, and they hadn't even started yet. How committed would he be? How much time did he intend to practice every day? There were too many unknowns. And what was a "few" years? Two? Three? Five?

"That's a tough one. Can I just pick a favorite number of

my own that isn't too difficult, and play it for you? If you work hard, you should be able to do this one in a few years."

Jillian selected a book and played a simple sonata by Mozart. "That's about the grade five Royal Conservatory level. Or would you rather hear something more contemporary?"

Jed's face lit up like a Christmas tree. "Wow," he mumbled as he scanned the open page. Jillian couldn't tell if he thought the written music looked too complicated or not. "Will I really be able to play like that?"

Jillian smiled, enjoying the opportunity to play for an appreciative student, rather than a parent who was merely listening to be polite. Although she had been asked to play piano for the worship service at church, she had declined, wanting to remain in the background. Never again would she be displayed in front of people, not even the moral and upright people at church. At least she knew the motives of her students, which was only to share her love of music and nothing more.

She started playing another selection at the same difficulty level. Jed lowered himself to her chair beside the piano. Out of the corner of her eye, she could see him leaning back, his long legs stretched out in front of him, smiling as she played, his eyes closed. She turned her concentration back to her music, before she completely lost her place.

At the closing diminuendo, his eyes opened and he continued to lie back, a lazy smile lingering on his face. Jillian tried to ignore her unwarranted impulse to smooth his hair.

"Do you really think I'll be able to play like that someday?"

She swallowed, mentally kicking herself for her thoughts. He was her student and nothing more. She swallowed hard and closed the book. "If you practice hard and keep at it, I don't see why not."

"Can you play me one more before my lesson? A favorite of yours? Do we have time?"

"Sure. This is called Moonlight Sonata."

The Beethoven classic was her current favorite, helping her to relax after a trying day. Jillian poured her heart into the music, and let the piano sing the melancholy melody. When she released the final chord, silence permeated the room.

"Wow, that was beautiful. You play as well as you teach." His starry-eyed smile made Jillian blush.

She cleared her throat. "Maybe we should get on with your lesson."

"Yeah, sure."

Jed sat beside her on the bench, and he proceeded to play the first two-line song without making a single mistake. Jillian tried not to be too impressed.

"Now play it again, and I'll play my part down here."

The duet sounded as good as could be expected for the first lesson in the book. All four songs progressed in the same manner, without error, and Jillian found herself hard-pressed not to grin at his enthusiasm, as well as his sense of humor about having to learn the easy beginner selections.

"I'm afraid that's it."

"Yup. Time for me to go get Betsy. See you next lesson."

They stood simultaneously, and she immediately missed his warmth.

"Yes, see you Tuesday, Jed." She didn't want to count the days until Tuesday. She accompanied him to the door.

Jed closed the door behind him and walked toward the school, trying to appear calm and carefree. He wondered if she was as curious about him as he was about her. And what was that book that was open on the piano, before she picked that classical number? He had been too far away to read the words, but the title of the song seemed like something he'd sung in church. He wondered how he could find out more about her.

But it didn't matter. Jed's smile turned to a hard frown. He'd learned his lessons the hard way, and he wasn't about to have a repeat performance. From now on, he would concentrate only on his lessons, not on his teacher.

three

"I can't play this!"

"But it's in the book. The book is progressive, and you should play everything in it, in the right order, for the maximum benefit from each lesson. Try it, you may even like it."

"I'm *not* playing 'Pop Goes the Weasel.' "

"You played 'Willy the Whale.' That one was fine."

Jed sat upright and folded his arms across his chest. "This is different. I'm a grown man. Grown men do not play 'Pop Goes the Weasel.' "

Jillian mumbled to herself, "And real men don't eat quiche." Up until now, Jed had progressed quickly with his lessons. An eager student, he had been more than prepared each lesson, even doing two lessons a week to hurry through the easy stuff at the beginning stages. In only a month and a half, they were nearly done with the first level.

"What did you say?" he asked.

"Nothing." She stopped to think for a minute. "If you play 'Pop Goes the Weasel' without making any mistakes after only one lesson, I'll promise not to tell anyone."

He balked. "Not good enough."

"Well, then I'll give you some homework on it. After you play the first part of the song, I want you to figure out the rest of it that isn't written in the book, and play the entire song for me next week. It's called 'playing by ear' and it's good for you."

"My mother is the only one that can tell me what's good for me," he groused.

"Jed." Jillian tapped her foot, but it had nothing to do with the beat of the music.

He grumbled under his breath again. "Mark was right. You are a slave driver."

Jillian narrowed her eyes to glare at him, but he returned her scowl with his dazzling white smile. She didn't smile back. He could turn on all the charm he wanted to, he wasn't going to *weasel* out of this one. And Jed really did know how to turn on the charm. Trouble was, she didn't think he was aware of it. Aside from a few jokes and some very short conversations, he kept personal details of his life as private as she did. She didn't know why, but it made her all the more curious about him, even though she kept telling herself she didn't want to know.

She tried to keep her mind on the lesson, where it belonged. "Tell you what. I'll play it first. I'm an adult, and I have no qualms about it. Listen."

Instead of merely leaning over to plunk out the beginner version from the book, Jillian rose from her chair, sat beside him on the piano bench, and played an embellished version of "Pop Goes the Weasel," exaggerating her demonstration with a rousing flourish of chord aggrandizement and brilliant accompaniment. Quite satisfied with her performance, Jillian folded her hands in her lap and turned to smile sweetly at him, hoping this would inspire him to greater things. His stupefied expression caused her to bite her lip to keep from laughing.

"You amaze me. Will I be able to do that someday?"

"I'm going to say the same thing I've said before. If you practice and work hard, then there is no reason why not. You just have to go through the book, learning each lesson step by step."

"Okay, you win. I'll play 'Pop Goes the Weasel.' But you still won't make me like it."

Jillian smiled back at him again. His beautiful smile always made her weaken. And the way his gorgeous blue eyes crinkled at the corners would send any woman's heart aflutter. Her eyes widened then narrowed at the direction of her thoughts, thoughts she refused to have ever again. "That's it," she said sternly.

He said the same thing at the end of every lesson. She followed every syllable in her thoughts as he spoke, almost mouthing his words. "Yup, time for me to go get Betsy."

As usual, she watched him walk down the street toward the school until he rounded the corner. Soon the selections in the book would become more difficult, and Jed would reach the point where each lesson would require enough work to keep him busy for a week. Trouble was, Jillian couldn't decide if that was good or bad.

❧

Busy making supper, Jed didn't notice Liz and Frank come in the door until he heard Liz's voice behind him, causing him to drop the spoon into the pot he was stirring.

"Hi, Jed." Liz peeked into one of the other pots as he tried to fish the spoon out with another one.

"Oh. Hi, Liz. Frank. How's work?"

Frank, as usual, said nothing. He disappeared into the living room to read the paper. Liz looked like she was sagging.

"I'm exhausted," she moaned. "I'm just glad it's Friday. You look quite perky, though. And what was that tune you were humming? Sounded like 'Pop Goes the Weasel.' "

❧

Jillian was gobbling down her lunch in the fifteen minutes she allotted on Saturday between morning and afternoon sessions, when the phone rang.

"Hello?" She answered the phone between bites, trying not to sound impatient. If she didn't finish her lunch before the next student arrived, she would go hungry. This job did not allow for coffee breaks. A trip to the bathroom proved equally difficult. But she couldn't let the answering machine get the phone, in case it was a student canceling his lesson.

Jed's cheerful voice rang out on the other end of the phone. "Hi, Jillian."

Jillian almost choked on the last bite of her sandwich. What was he doing calling on Saturday? After the scene he made yesterday, she hoped he wasn't phoning to complain about "Pop Goes the Weasel." "Yes, Jed, what can I do for you?"

"I know you're trying to rush down your lunch, so I won't keep you. I was wondering if you'd like to join me for dinner tonight after your lessons for the day are over."

Dinner? Like a date? The thought of Jed asking her out hadn't crossed her mind as a possibility. "I'm really in a hurry before my next student gets here, so I don't have time to talk about it, but my answer is no. I don't date my students."

Jed paused only briefly. "I'm not asking for a date. I'm just asking if you would like to join me for dinner. I'm bored and lonely, and I was hoping you'd feel sorry for me."

Jillian checked her watch, counting the seconds. Her next student was due to arrive any moment. "No, Jed, I don't think so." She estimated she had one minute to gulp down her milk and run to the bathroom.

"Aw, come on. I'm all alone and I don't even know where to go in this town."

Jillian heard the sound of a car stopping and cutting the engine. "I don't think it's a good idea." The car door slammed. Then another.

"Aw, come on. Please? I promise to behave."

The doorbell rang. Jillian glanced toward the door and shuffled her feet. "Oh, all right. I'll be finished at six o'clock. And I'll need a few minutes to get ready."

"Sounds great. I won't keep you. Bye." A click sounded as he hung up.

"Bye," Jillian answered to dead-air space, mentally kicking herself as she replaced the receiver. She wondered if he questioned her excuse about not dating her students. Would he know the oldest of her students, except for himself, was only fifteen and female?

She literally ran to answer the door for her first student of the afternoon, but found it difficult to concentrate on the lesson. If it wasn't a date, then what was it when a man invited a woman out to dinner on Saturday night? And the next time she considered a date, she would be sure she knew the man and he came with full recommendations from at least ten reliable sources. She knew nothing about Jed and practically nothing about his family, other than one of her other students was his nephew, and they paid on time. At the sound of a horrible discord, she focused her full attention on her student, where it should have been in the first place.

Jed arrived on time at 6:00. However, her lessons were running a bit late, so Jed sat waiting in the hallway in the chair reserved for incoming students. Even though he remained quiet, she could see him out of the corner of her eye, and she found him distracting. Like a typical man, Jed sat with his long legs stretched out in front of him and slightly apart as he leaned back in the seat with his hands casually clasped behind his head, the picture of lazy contentment. How could a man with such masculine appeal be so. . .nice?

Jillian tried her best to concentrate on the broken and uneven performance of her student. "I think that needs a bit more practice, Deborah, but you've come a long way in one week. What do you think?"

"Yes," Deborah replied. "I've been working on the hard parts, but I should have it better for next week."

"Next week, then. Our time is up. Keep up the good work."

"Thank you, Miss Jefferson, I will."

With that, Jillian closed the book and the girl picked it up, prepared to leave. Jed straightened in the chair but did not stand as Jillian saw her student to the door. When the door closed, they stared at each other, neither of them speaking. Jillian's mouth refused to move as a million thoughts raced through her mind. If the only reason she had agreed to accompany him to dinner was because he had badgered her into it, why did she look forward to the evening so much? The thought scared her.

Jed stood. "Are you hungry? I have no idea where to go in this city, so it's up to you to pick someplace good."

Jillian composed her thoughts. "Sure. I just have to freshen up and I'll be right back."

She walked stiffly to the bathroom, trying to hold herself properly, in case he was watching her. After a few composing breaths, she checked her reflection in the mirror. She wore no makeup and her hair was a mess. Although her hair was naturally wavy, she would have liked to run a curling iron through it, but she didn't have time with Jed waiting. Then she wondered why it mattered. Jed was a student, nothing more. She brushed her hair to fluff it up and hastily applied a little lipstick.

Trying to quell her jitters, she rummaged through her box of earrings, but ended up simply wearing the ones she already had on. This wasn't a date. She was Jed's teacher, and it was only dinner, and she had no intention of trying to impress him. She stood back to give herself one final check in the mirror.

Jed wiped his sweaty palms on his pants, although he didn't know why he was nervous. As it was, he still didn't know why he'd asked her in the first place. He wasn't sure he could trust his own judgment anymore, but after nearly two months of piano lessons and pumping Mark with questions, he'd decided to take a chance that Jillian was safe.

He made his decision based on the fact that even though they enjoyed each other's company during lesson time, she'd made herself perfectly clear on many occasions that she had no interest in him other than as a student, which was fine with him. Jed tried to convince himself that was exactly what he wanted, although the thought stung, just a little.

And to top it off, now Liz was mad at him because they'd hardly spent any time alone together since he got here. If she found out he was taking the piano teacher out tonight instead of her, she'd hit the roof. The guys from work had invited him out for a couple of beers, too. And here he was, standing in Jillian's front hall, shuffling his feet like a kid on his first date.

Jillian stepped out into the hall and sucked in a deep breath. "I guess I'm as ready as I'll ever be." She still wondered about the wisdom of seeing Jed outside of lessons, but his teasing sense of humor made her laugh like no one else, and against her better judgment, she looked forward to an evening with him.

Unlike Graham, Jed never tried to impress her, or made promises he had no intention of keeping. And why was she comparing Jed to Graham? Jillian clenched her teeth. She had no intention of dating Jed. Ever.

Jed removed his jacket from the coatrack and slung it over his shoulder. "Let's go."

Jillian slipped her feet into the nearest pair of shoes, speaking without raising her head. "I'm not so sure this is a good idea, Jed," she mumbled. The last time she let her guard down she had met with disastrous results, and she refused to let that happen again. She enjoyed Jed's company too much to risk crossing that line.

She sensed a lack of movement from Jed as he stood with his hand on the doorknob. "It's just dinner. Relax, Jillian. We can discuss the intricacies of 'Pop Goes the Weasel' if you want, but I'd prefer we didn't."

Discussing "Pop Goes the Weasel" was the furthest thing from her mind, but she would if she had to. A knot formed in her gut, and she wondered exactly what they would discuss; her suspicion that this really wasn't a good idea solidified into certainty. What did she know about him, except that he could carry on with amiable chitchat, and that he really was serious about learning to play the piano, at least so far? However, it was too late to back out now, so she would make the best of the evening. She would have dinner with Jed, and from that point on, she would only see him during lessons.

Jillian sighed in relief at her sensible conclusion. "Shall we go?"

After she locked the door, she followed Jed to a huge, snappy four-wheel-drive truck parked in front of her house. She realized that since he walked to every lesson, she hadn't known what kind of car he drove, or if he even owned one. Now she knew.

She grasped the door frame and hoisted herself way up into it, swishing her long flowing skirt underneath her as she scrambled onto the seat. "Nice truck," she commented, fishing for something to open a safe topic of conversation. Personally, she preferred her economy compact car, which was much closer to the ground. Why did men pick vehicles you needed a ladder to get into?

Jed watched Jillian struggle to climb into the passenger seat. He could tell she wasn't impressed with his truck, but after all that had happened recently, it was the only material goods he had to his name besides a few pieces of furniture. He wasn't even sure she was very impressed with him, either.

He walked around to the driver's side. She couldn't have made her intentions any more clear, and it hurt. But wasn't that what he wanted? To stay clear of any close personal involvement? He was going to need a whole year of careful managing to recover from what Brenda had done to him, and he didn't want to go through that again, emotionally or financially. Nothing was going to stop him from fulfilling his dream this time. Nothing. Including and especially Jillian Jefferson.

four

The roar of the engine startled Jillian as Jed turned the key to start the large truck. He stepped on the clutch, threw the stick shift into gear, and turned to her. "So, where should we go?"

She directed him through the city as Jed good-naturedly complained about the traffic, as if he had to worry driving his huge monstrosity of a truck. One of the few things she knew about him was that he had previously lived in a small town in northern British Columbia, and she wondered if it even had rush hour traffic.

As she expected, a line awaited them when they arrived at the restaurant. Jed added their names to the waiting list, and Jillian wondered what to do to kill time until it came their turn for a table.

She had enjoyed his lighthearted banter in the truck, even his teasing about her height and her difficulty climbing into the high cab. Jillian struggled to think of a way to get back at him.

As a popular piano tune came on the background music, an idea came to her. "So, seen any weasels lately?" she asked, humming his favorite song, just to get his goat.

He quirked one eyebrow in response. "Yeah, but I chased it around a bush in the backyard for fun, then I popped him. He's gone now."

The hostess chose that moment to call their names, preventing Jillian from making a reply.

As they were seated, another waiter delivered a colorful castle-shaped kids-meal box to the family at the next table. The child delved into it, going for the ice cream first before the mother removed the container from his tiny fingers and placed it in the center of the table. The child complained at the same time as he started to shovel the fries into his mouth.

Jed sighed as he watched. "Mark and Betsy would love it here," he said.

"I've been wondering why you're doing that."

"Doing what?"

"Baby-sitting." Jillian studied Jed as he sat across from her. Tall, good-looking, intelligent, and single. And he had a job, so he wasn't desperate for money. While she was curious, lesson time was not the time for such a personal question. Even though it was probably none of her business, she'd wondered from the first time she met him why he was baby-sitting.

"Well, they're not exactly babies. Mark is in grade three, and Betsy is in kindergarten. They're just not old enough to be left alone. It's not bad, although I must admit sometimes they do drive me a little nuts. That's why I decided to take piano lessons." He grinned and winked. Jillian nearly choked on her water.

"So you decided to take piano lessons to help keep you sane." Now she had an answer to that question, which only led her to wonder about other things. "You still haven't explained why you're doing baby-sitting."

"It's not really a very exciting story." He shrugged his shoulders. "When the mill where I worked shut down, I sold my condo and managed to find a job here in town. At the same time, my sister's sitter quit. Seems she thinks it's cheaper to have me live there than pay for day care. She asked me if I would baby-sit in exchange for room and board until next September. They feed me, except I have to start supper on weekdays. So here I am. End of story."

"Why September? That's nearly a year away. What's happening in September?"

Jed's back stiffened. "I've registered for college, and I'm going to finish up my degree in education."

"Education? I thought you had a job." Jillian had no teaching degrees. Of course she had her bachelor's degree in music, but she'd never taken any teaching courses.

"I plan to be a high school teacher. I'm going to teach English."

Jillian imagined a string of giddy teenage girls hanging around Jed after class. The boys would probably suffer from slight cases of hero-delusions as well. As it was, Mark worshipped the ground Jed walked on. She heard a little more about Jed every Tuesday during Mark's lesson. She would have liked Jed even if she had never met him. According to Mark, not only could he cook, but he wasn't afraid of housework. She imagined women waiting in line for him.

Her lips tightened as she stopped her mind from wandering. She would not be waiting in line, picking a number.

"So, what do you do besides piano lessons, your night job, and baby-sitting?"

"Not much. I don't get out much." Jed paused and started to play with his silverware. "I hope there isn't something or someone I'm keeping you from tonight."

Jillian would have laughed, except it wasn't funny. Aside from piano lessons, her calendar was bare. If he was referring to the possibility of a boyfriend, he couldn't be more wrong. The men who asked her for a date only wanted one thing, and when she didn't give in, they were no longer interested in her. She had simply stopped opening herself up to more disappointments, and she was happy that way.

She sighed, then caught her breath, hoping Jed hadn't noticed. At first, she had thought Graham was different, but in the end, the wounds he inflicted were worse than all of them combined. "No, the opposite, I'm afraid to admit. Since

I decided to teach piano lessons for a living, most of my evenings are taken up, and by the time Saturday night rolls around, I'm usually too tired to go out."

The waiter arrived with their orders, halting their conversation for the moment. At first she was hesitant, but she made a quick decision to bow her head for a few seconds of silent prayer before she ate. The same split second her eyes closed, Jed's hand touched her wrist. Her eyes shot open.

"Jillian? Are you doing what I think you're doing?"

Her head lowered again. "I just paused for a moment of thanks," she mumbled.

"Can we pray together?"

Her heart caught in her throat. She knew Mark's family attended church, but she didn't know if Jed also participated in church life, nor did she know the depth of his commitment, or if it included praying in a public restaurant. Not only that, she wasn't sure she was ready to pray with him, because praying with someone encouraged a closeness she didn't want to share with Jed. But she couldn't refuse without looking churlish. She gulped and nodded.

Jed bowed his head. "Thank You, Heavenly Father, for this time of fellowship, this good meal, and the abundance You provide for us. Amen."

All she could do was raise her head, blink, and stare.

His ears reddened as he reached for his fork. "Hey, with two hungry little kids waiting to eat, we don't do long prayers. Don't you hate when you go out after church, and by the time the prayer is finished, your lunch is cold?"

"I guess."

Jed caught her off guard with his wide smile, starting to eat and continuing on as if there had been no interruption. "So, if you don't get out much, how would you like to have lunch together sometime during the week? I drop Betsy off at 12:30

every day, and don't have to pick her up until 3:00. Or maybe we could do something else, although to tell the truth, I still haven't figured out what there is to do in the afternoon. I usually do my share of the housework, and practice my piano lessons like a good boy." He finished off his statement with an exaggerated wink.

Jillian turned her head down and mumbled into her plate. "There's not too much to do during the day." All she did during the day was housework, shopping when necessary, and occasional visits with her sister.

Jed grinned back at her, his bright blue eyes flashing. "Well, maybe we could play tennis, or go for a walk or something. I don't know. I'm open to suggestions."

She almost said no, but the more she thought about it, the less appeal lonely afternoons held compared to spending the time with Jed. Since teaching piano lessons involved sitting for hours, the possibility of a little exercise sounded better and better. Tennis seemed a little extreme, especially since it was nearly Christmas, but she was open to suggestions. "A walk sounds nice. Sometimes I go out to walk around the mall, just to get out and moving around."

"If you like to walk, we're about finished here. Want to go for a walk now?"

Jillian checked her watch. "Now? It's dark out."

Jed smiled that dazzling white smile she was growing so fond of. "It seems like a nice neighborhood, and it's not raining. Unlike you people who were born and raised in the Vancouver area, I'm used to icy cold and being up to my armpits in snow this time of year. And don't worry about it being dark; I don't think anyone will bother us. Don't forget, you'll have Little Jed to keep you safe. And if you don't think I can protect you, we can borrow my sister's dog."

The comment about "Little Jed" made her smile. The

casualness of his attitude completely disarmed her, so she pretended to consider it. "Hmm. . ." She tapped her index finger to her chin. "Maybe. What kind of dog?"

Jed covered his heart with his palm and pretended to look hurt, making Jillian wonder if he'd ever taken acting lessons. "You'd pick the dog for protection over me?"

"Depends. Is it a Doberman?"

"It's a mutt. A Heinz 57, mixed-heritage mongrel. An ordinary, hairy brown dog."

His ridiculous hangdog expression made her snicker. "You win. Let's go for a walk. Without the dog."

Jed paid the bill, and they left. Jillian gazed out the window the entire drive back to her house. Stars shone overhead in the clear sky. The air was nippy, but it was still above freezing. She supposed she was spoiled, never having lived anywhere else. There had been some snow last winter, but it barely covered the ground and was gone within a day. And unlike most people, she had the luxury of not having to worry about driving to work in it, and Jillian liked it that way.

Jed locked his door, pocketed the keys, and ran around to Jillian's side. "Ready?"

Still seated in the truck, she looked both ways down the block. "Where do you want to go?" she asked. Not that it really mattered.

He raised his hands in the air, then flopped them down to his sides. "Anywhere but to the school."

Jillian couldn't help but giggle as Jed held out his hand to help her out. Against her better judgment, his playful expression made her take his hand. "Then I guess we go that way." She pointed.

He didn't let go of her as they started to walk, and rather than protest over something so silly, she allowed him to hold her hand as they walked slowly and wordlessly down the street. They walked in silence, the only sounds being the clicking of her heels on the cement and the drone of the odd car in the distance.

When they approached a playground, Jed stopped. "Want to go for a swing?" He held out one arm in the direction of a large metal swing set.

Jillian checked from side to side, then up at him. "Us? Now?"

"Yeah, sure. Why not?"

Jillian studied the swings. She hadn't been on a swing in years, and at this hour, no one would see them. She could almost feel the brush of air on her face and the rush of weightlessness.

She nearly gave in to temptation, but good sense overruled. "I don't think so. I can't go on a swing in a skirt." However, Jillian's gaze remained glued to the vacant swings.

"Just wrap your skirt underneath you, and you'll be fine. I'll bet you haven't been on a swing in years." Jed smiled down at her, and she looked up, her gaze fixed on his eyes. He squeezed her hand, then released the pressure. "Come on, it'll be fun. I'll push you. . . ." His voice trailed off as his smile widened.

Jillian's heart fluttered in her chest. He was right: it had been years since she'd been on a swing. As a girl, she'd enjoyed many solitary hours swinging. She hesitated. If she gave in, no one would see. Forgetting the dignified image she tried so hard to uphold, she dropped his hand and ran to the swing

Tucking her skirt underneath her as much as she could, she wiggled her bottom into the rubber seat. "All set!" Jillian held the chain tightly and tilted her head backward, unable to wipe the smile off her face as Jed grasped the chain and pulled her back.

"Ready?"

"Ready!" Jillian held her breath as he pulled her further back and held her suspended for a few moments.

"Go!" With Jed's firm but gentle push, Jillian dipped down, then swung up, exhilarated by the feeling of weightlessness before she drifted down and back again with the swing.

Jillian wiggled her feet as Jed continued to push her while she swung gaily back and forth. Stopping at the swings had turned out to be a great idea, something she never would have considered doing. She closed her eyes as she neared the top, then opened them and tilted her head back as she started to descend, floating backward to have Jed push her higher.

Feeling as free as a child, suspended for that brief moment in time before she drifted backward and down again, Jillian sucked in a deep breath of the cool air and kicked her feet. One shoe went flying off. "Oh no! Stop! Jed! My shoe!"

As she floated back, Jed's hands grasped her by the hips, lowering her to a halt. Thankfully, he couldn't see her blush in the darkness. With any luck, he would stay behind her while she looked for her errant shoe.

She leaned forward to hop off, but Jed didn't let her go. "Don't step in the sand in your stockings. I'll find it. What color is it?"

Jillian held out the foot with the shoe still on it. "Well, this one is blue, so the one that fell must be the same. I realize that there must be lots of shoes out there, so knowing the color is dreadfully important."

Jed stood in front of her and gave her a comical dirty look but said nothing.

"Really, Jed," she chided him. "Ask a stupid question, you get a stupid answer."

"It wasn't a stupid question. If I was looking for a tan shoe the same color as the sand it would be impossible to find in the dark. If I was looking for a black shoe, it would be easy to find, and if I was looking for a white shoe, it would only be marginally difficult."

"Jed, it's December."

"What? So?"

"You can't wear white shoes past Labor Day."

"Oh? Excuse me. Who wrote that rule?"

"It's been in effect since the beginning of time."

Jed mumbled something under his breath as he continued to look for the missing shoe in the dark. "Found it," he called, shaking the sand out of it as he walked toward her. Instead of handing it to her, he bent down on one knee, picked up her foot, rubbed his thumb in a massaging motion along her instep, then slid the shoe onto her foot. He grinned up at her and then bowed. "Cinderella," he said with a grin and a slight nod.

Jillian gulped. She wanted to say *Prince Charming* but couldn't speak the words. He'd turned what would have been a dull evening into a fairy-tale night, bringing back a child-hood simplicity she had long forgotten.

Jed stood and backed up a step. "Don't kick your feet this time, okay? Don't think I didn't notice you kicking your feet."

He walked behind her again to pull her back with another gentle push, starting her off again. After a few more pushes, Jillian drifted back and forth at a comfortable height, restraining herself from kicking her feet.

A movement caught her attention. Jed whooshed past, riding the swing beside her, gaining more height with every repetition, until he was slightly higher than she was.

"Watch this!" he called out. As the swing reached the highest point, Jed jumped. "Bonzai!" he yelled, flying through the air with his hands and legs spread-eagle. He landed on his feet, continuing the momentum with a single somersault, and then stopped, standing with his hands raised high in the air.

He turned around and bowed dramatically, grinning from ear to ear. "I knew I could still do it!"

Jillian feared her heart would pound through her chest. She clutched the chain with a death grip, forcing herself to gulp for air. When Jed went flying into the air like a reckless kid, all she could see was the image of him breaking his neck while she was helpless to do anything about it. And he had the nerve to be proud of himself.

She cleared her throat to find her voice. "Are you crazy?" she squeaked out. "You could have killed yourself doing a stupid stunt like that!"

"Hey, I knew what I was doing!" The silly grin remained while he shrugged his shoulders. "I've done this a million times!"

Jillian continued to drift back and forth on the swing, not sure she could find the strength in her legs to drag herself to a stop. "And how old were you?"

He stood before her and laughed. "I don't know. Fourteen?"

Jillian didn't feel the least little bit like laughing. She felt like wringing his fool neck, the same neck he could just as easily have broken. "And you obviously haven't grown up since then."

"Hey! I wouldn't have even thought of doing that in front of the kids." He shrugged his shoulders, then rammed his hands into his pockets. "Bad example and all that stuff. Besides, you're just jealous. I'll bet it's something you've been dying to do and are too afraid to try."

"I am not!"

"Chicken." He had the nerve to cluck.

"I'm not chicken."

"Prove it."

"Don't dare me, mister."

"Me? I would never dare you to do anything."

Jillian said nothing. His attitude alone was a dare. It was dark. No one would ever know.

"I'll catch you." Jed planted his legs firmly apart and held out his arms, waiting in an open invitation.

"If you drop me, I'll never forgive you."

"I found your shoe, didn't I?"

Jillian wondered what that had to do with anything as she pumped herself up higher.

"Here I come!" And with that, Jillian slid to the edge of the seat, stuffed her skirt between her knees, and pushed herself off. "Bonzai!" she called out. Time stretched in the exhilarating rush of being suspended in midair, and down she went.

True to his word, Jed caught her with no difficulty. Solid as a rock, he stood firmly rooted to one spot, catching her with ease. Slowly and gently, he lowered her to the ground, gripping her firmly around the waist. Jillian's breath caught in her throat at the contact. He smiled down at her as her feet touched ground, and Jillian tried to convince herself that the increase in her breathing was from the excitement of the leap, not the landing.

Grateful that the darkness would hide the color she knew rose in her cheeks, she bent to smooth any crinkles from her skirt. "Well," she mumbled, "both shoes are still on my feet."

Jed apparently didn't notice her discomfort. "Want to try bungee jumping next? I hear it's fun."

Jillian patted her hair down. "I don't think so, Jed. This little daredevil adventure should keep me satisfied for the next ten or so years. And we should go. If we make any more noise, someone is going to call the cops. We both live in this neighborhood." She lowered her voice. "Besides, I have to get up early for church in the morning."

Jed sighed. "Yeah," he mumbled. "Me too."

Careful to avoid his hand, Jillian walked beside Jed in

silence the whole way back to her house. She would have to reconsider future dealings with Jed. As a student, she could ignore him, but as a Christian, she didn't know which way to turn. Her head told her that she would be safe to trust him, but her heart told her that her higher expectations would only lead to bigger disappointments.

She unlocked her front door and pocketed her keys. As she pushed the door open, Jed's soft voice murmured into her ear. "Can I see you again tomorrow?"

"I don't think so, Jed." Part of her wanted to tell him to wait until his next lesson, but part of her didn't want to wait that long.

"Lunch Monday?"

Jillian opened her mouth to protest, but the wrong words came out. "Sure. Lunch Monday sounds fine."

She waited for Jed to politely say good night, but instead, he lifted her hand to his lips and kissed it.

"Good night, Jillian, see you Monday. And think about bungee jumping; you're a natural."

Before she could properly unscramble her thoughts, he turned, strode to his truck, and drove off.

Jillian stood on her doorstep, staring at the huge truck until it rounded the corner. What had happened? The prim and proper piano teacher had just jumped screaming from a swing into a man's arms at midnight—and enjoyed it. Her heart still pounded from his small kiss to her hand! Was he doing this on purpose?

She shook her head, reminding herself of what was bound to happen if she let things continue. Next lesson she would make it clear that they would not see each other except for lesson time.

Next lesson, she would talk to him. Unfortunately that would be after the lunch date she had already promised him.

five

Only the living room lamp was on, and that was on the lowest setting. Jed sucked in a deep breath as he gently inserted the key in the lock and turned it, praying the rumble of his truck hadn't woken the dog. And if that hadn't, surely the key would. He gritted his teeth as Missy scratched the door, but fortunately the dog didn't bark. She had taken a month before she stopped barking at him when he arrived home from work at 2:00 in the morning, and now instead, she jumped on him and showered him with wet dog kisses. Jed didn't know which was worse.

He shucked off his cowboy boots and pushed them into the row of shoes beside the door with his foot. As strange as it had been at the beginning, he kind of liked the feeling of not living alone. He'd had his own condominium for almost four years, but living alone, it had never felt like home.

He patted the dog to quiet her whining and tiptoed downstairs to the den, which was now his bedroom. Between the double bed, dresser, stereo, and his large television, he could barely move, but it was home.

Once he tucked himself in bed, he couldn't sleep, even though he was tired. The evening had not progressed like he'd expected. He might have had a few ideas of his own before he arrived at Jillian's house, but if God had other plans, it wouldn't be the first time. The way things had turned out threw him for a loop.

Jed lay on his back in the dark, staring at the ceiling. What had come over him to act like that? Normally, he was a pretty responsible, respectable kind of guy. Whatever had possessed him to jump off the swing? He was a little too old to be showing off, but young enough to get carried away.

He covered his eyes with his forearm. Why had he kissed her hand like that? He could tell by her reaction that he'd surprised her, but he'd surprised himself even more: He'd been on the swings in the park at midnight with Jillian Jefferson, the piano teacher.

Jillian. He sighed and rolled over onto his stomach. What should he do? During lesson time, Jillian always remained quiet and reserved, but this evening proved what he had suspected all along. Underneath that prim and proper teacher lay a woman full of wit and whimsy. Warm and responsive, she'd held his hand. And she was a believer.

Jillian was hard to resist, but resist he must. He'd fallen for Brenda, but in the end, she'd squandered everything he had to give her, and more. If it hadn't been for Brenda, he would already be in college, but instead, if he worked hard enough all year, he might be able to start next September. He wasn't going to let himself be in the position ever again where a woman made a fool of him. Not that Jillian would ever be so devious. She had too much dignity to do what Brenda had done.

Dignity? Was he referring to the woman who jumped off a swing at midnight? With those high heels, if he hadn't caught her properly, she could have been hurt.

He smiled at the memory of holding her before he lowered her to the ground. Fortunately, the cover of darkness had prevented her from seeing his expression. At the time, he was sure he had been wearing his heart on his sleeve, something he couldn't afford. His last experience had cost him a year off his life and a piece of his heart, and he wasn't willing to chance a repeat performance.

He would get together with Jillian to have lunch only because he had already promised, and then he wouldn't see her except for lesson time.

Jed finally fell asleep, dreaming about sharing a swing in the dark, accompanied by soft strains of gentle piano music in the background.

&

Luckily, Jillian arrived at the coffee shop at the same time as Sue. Church had been late getting out, and she hated the thought of leaving Sue waiting. They picked a table against the window and settled in, ready to enjoy a quiet couple of hours without Sue's four children.

"Enjoying the peace and quiet?" Jillian asked her frazzled sister, already knowing the answer.

Sue rolled her eyes, then turned her attention to her donut. "I can't stay as long as usual. I have to do some shopping without the kids. I hate Christmas shopping, but I'm almost done, record early, too, if I can find what I want. Are you going to walk around the mall with me after we finish our coffee?"

Jillian groaned. "I went for a walk yesterday, and like a fool, I was in my high heels. My feet are killing me!"

Sue licked the whipped cream off the top of her donut, closing her eyes for a second to savor it. When she opened her eyes again, she stared unwavering, straight into Jillian's face. "What's his name?"

Jillian nearly choked on her coffee. "Whose name?"

"The tall man you went out with yesterday." Sue sucked a dribble of chocolate icing off the tip of one finger.

Jillian's cheeks reddened. "Did you have spies out after me or something?"

"You're so transparent, Jillian; you always have been. I could tell from your face that it was a man, and when you admitted you wore high heels, I knew he was tall or else you would have worn something more practical. Then when you said your feet were sore, I knew it was a long walk, so I know it has to be serious. I didn't get my Big Sister Certificate for nothing."

They both smiled, remembering the gag gift Jillian gave to Sue on Mother's Day—a certificate for excellency in the role of big sister. When their parents divorced, their mother remarried, but her new husband didn't want children from a previous marriage around, so they lived with their father, who really hadn't wanted to be bothered with children either. Seven years older, Sue had been as much a mother to Jillian as a sister, and now they were inseparable.

Jillian swirled the last bit of coffee around in the bottom of her cup, studying it as it swished. "He's actually one of my students, Mark Edwards' uncle. And yes, he's tall. We went for a walk last night, that's all." She purposely missed telling Sue about holding Jed's hand, or about how she jumped off the swing into his arms. And she didn't want to make too much out of Jed's kissing her hand. Just thinking about it, though, gave her goose bumps.

Sue licked her fingers again after finishing the last bite of her donut. "You're avoiding telling me about him. Now I know it's serious. And you really should have had one of those donuts. They're fabulous. Now are you going to come with me or not?"

"I don't know how you stay so skinny, eating all that junk. You make me jealous, you know. And yes, of course I'm going with you around the mall. You shouldn't even have to ask, if I'm so transparent. Besides," Jillian winked, "I need more stickers for my students."

Sue sighed. "Always the dedicated teacher. On your only day off, yet."

"I can't help it. How many people could say they love their

job as much as I do? And working from my home, too."

Sue snorted as she reached under the table for her purse. "Let's go. If we find what I need quickly, we can come back for another donut."

Even though it usually meant shopping, Jillian always enjoyed her sister's company. However, on Sunday, Jillian would have preferred seeing her sister and her family in church. Although Sue respected Jillian's beliefs, she didn't see a need for God in her own life, and she refused to discuss it. Graham had claimed to be a Christian, which hadn't helped Jillian's efforts to share her faith with Sue. In fact, it was something else in her life that Graham had destroyed.

Jillian's only consolation was to occasionally take Sue's kids to Sunday school with her, hoping some of it would rub off on her sister, except deep down she knew Sue only agreed in order to get some time alone with her husband.

Of course, Jillian continued to pray for Sue and her family daily, praying from the depths of her soul that Sue could find the same peace that God had given her.

They walked and walked until Sue found all the items she needed, and Jillian collected enough reward stickers to replenish her stockpile. True to her word, Sue made sure they finished their excursion back at the coffee shop where she purchased another donut. Jillian meant only to have another coffee, but caved in and ordered a donut as well.

"So, when are you going out on another date?"

"It wasn't a date, Sue. It was just a walk."

Sue rolled her eyes again. "Yeah, sure."

Jillian's face paled at Sue's use of Jed's favorite expression. She tried to act calm and pass it off. "I'm not dating him. He's just a student. Nothing more."

"I'm not dating him," Sue playfully mocked, then stuffed another piece of donut into her mouth. "I used that same line when I was dating Geoff, and I married him in the end. But suit yourself. I don't know who you think you're fooling."

Sue knew her too well, but this time Sue was wrong.

"He feels the same way. We're only going to see each other at lesson time." She dropped her voice to a whisper. "And lunch tomorrow," she mumbled.

Sue laughed as she gulped down the last of her coffee and checked her watch. "I gotta run. See you next week. Have a nice lunch date."

છે

The flashing message light greeted Jillian upon her return home from the mall. Jed's cheery voice inquired whether she would be interested in joining him for a burger if she got home in time for supper.

This would be a good opportunity to tell Jed that she didn't want to see him except for lessons. She looked up the number and called him. Mark answered the phone.

"Can I speak to your uncle Jed, please?"

She heard muffled scraping as Mark put one hand over the phone, but his scream still pierced her eardrums. "Uncle Jed, it's for you! It's Miss Jefferson! Uncle Jed! Miss Jefferson wants to talk to you!"

Jillian winced. Now the entire household knew who was calling for Jed. She heard a muffled click as Jed picked up the extension phone.

Jillian's eardrums nearly burst again when Jed yelled. "I've got it! You can hang up now, Mark!" Through the ringing in her ears, another click sounded. Jed's smooth and cheery voice came on in a lower volume. "Hi! I see you got my message."

After the big production with the entire household, Jillian didn't want to tell him her decision over the phone. She would tell him away from prying eyes and curious ears. Her stomach rumbled, one donut and two cups of strong coffee being a poor substitution for a decent lunch. Jed's original offer began to gather appeal. "Yes, is it too late to take you up on that burger?"

"Not at all. We haven't eaten yet. Have you?"

"No."

"And how do you feel about catching a movie after? We'll still have time."

"Catch a movie?" She paused to think. She had already committed herself to the burger. She tried to stall to give herself time to think. "Depends on how fast it's going, I suppose."

Jed's soft chuckle made her heart flutter. "I'll be over as quick as I can then, so it won't get away. See you in a few minutes. Bye."

Even though he chided himself for being slightly rude by hanging up so fast, Jed patted himself on the back for ending the conversation before Jillian had the chance to change her mind. The second he hung up the phone, Jed dashed into the bathroom. He rubbed his chin and shaved for the second time that day, not that she would get close enough to notice. He applied a little gel to his unruly hair, and decided he needed a haircut. Tomorrow.

He stepped back to look at himself, running his hand over the faded picture on his T-shirt. Not classy. He ran back to his bedroom and selected a crisp cotton shirt, which might have been a little on the dressy side for a burger and a show, but it felt nice and looked good with his new jeans. Making one last check to make sure the kids hadn't smeared anything on them, he tucked in his shirt and vaulted down the stairs, straight for the family room.

Liz and Frank's heads turned in unison away from the television as he rummaged through the pile of newspapers, searching for the movie section of Saturday's paper.

"I won't be home for dinner," he mumbled as he pulled the paper out of the pile.

"Well, you sure look nice, Jed. Where are you going?" Liz asked.

"Oh," he mumbled, trying to avoid the issue. "Nowhere special, just out for a burger with Jillian. When was the last time you took some papers out to the recycling bin?"

"Jillian? Jillian who?" Liz's voice trailed off. She blinked, then sat straight up on the couch. "Do you mean Miss Jefferson, the piano teacher? Is that why she called you? To ask you out for a burger?"

"Uh, yeah, something like that."

Jed pulled the movie page out of the middle of the paper. "Got it. Don't wait up for me. Bye." He ran out, leaving his sister with her mouth hanging open and one finger in the air.

❧

Jillian rummaged through her closet, frantically searching for the right thing to wear. She wanted something attractive but not too fancy, yet comfortable enough to sit in at the theater. Since Jed said he'd be right over, she didn't have a second to waste.

On an impulse, she picked a baggy pink sweater and a snug short denim skirt, yanked them on, then ran into the bathroom to touch up her makeup and comb out her hair. She stepped back to study herself in the mirror. A little spritz of perfume, and she'd be ready.

The second she sprayed the perfume, she regretted it. Why was she in such a tizzy to get ready? After dinner, she planned to tell Jed that she didn't want to see him except for lesson time.

Jillian stared at her reflection in the mirror. The last time she got all in a fluff about getting ready for a man was for Graham, and in the end he was more concerned with the outward package than the person within. In going through all this effort to look her best, she was perpetuating the trend. With that thought in mind, Jillian had filled the sink to wash off the makeup when the doorbell rang.

Jed stood at the door, waiting, his heart pounding. What was he doing? Yesterday he'd given himself a good speech about not getting involved in a relationship, but he'd lain awake half the night thinking of Jillian. He tried to convince himself he only had one reason for asking her to dinner, and that was to avoid getting out of the house alone.

Jillian opened the door, and Jed thought he'd been hit in the chest with a sledgehammer.

"Hi, Jed. That was quick. I barely had enough time to get ready."

His mouth opened, then closed before he said something to make himself look like a drooling idiot. Between the dark but subtle makeup accents on her eyes and the muted-colored lipstick, she had transformed from moderately beautiful to drop-dead gorgeous.

He shoved his hands in his pockets. "Yeah, I see you're ready."

"Did you get a haircut?"

Jed ran his hand over his hair with a nervous laugh. "It's amazing what a little gel will do, isn't it?"

She clasped her hands in front of her in a gesture so feminine and sweet, Jed had to struggle not to reach out and touch her.

"Where are we going?" she asked. "Or do you want me to decide?"

Jed couldn't have decided if his life depended on it. The way his thoughts were running, he should have headed straight for the evening service at church. "It's your neighborhood. You pick. Or maybe we should go inside and choose a movie now, so we know how much time we have first."

"I'm afraid I didn't pick up the weekend paper. I have no

idea what's playing."

Jed pulled the folded-up movie page out of his jacket pocket. "I brought it from home. I wasn't sure if you would have it or not."

"Good idea. Come on in."

He thought he could finally relax when she turned and walked into the house—but she looked just as good in back as she did in front. As he followed her past the piano and into the kitchen, he gritted his teeth and reminded himself she was his piano teacher.

They spread the movie page on the table. They didn't take long to agree on a comedy they'd both seen a preview of on television. Jed tore their selection out and stuffed it in his jacket pocket. Standing, he held out his hand to her. "Let's go. I'm starving."

"Jed, why did you call me?"

Jed couldn't stop his cheeks from heating up. He shrugged his shoulders, trying to act casual. He really didn't know why he'd called, because he had told himself he was going to avoid her. "Liver," he said lamely.

She grimaced. "Liver?"

"Yeah, Liz is making liver for supper, and I'd have to eat it and act like I liked it in front of the kids. I do a lot of things for those kids, but I refuse to do that." He placed one palm in the center of his chest and held the other in the air. "As a Christian, I'm not supposed to lie."

Jillian tried not to smile at his imitation of a boy scout. For one thing, he was twice the height of any scouts she'd ever seen, and for another thing, boy scouts didn't wink. Unable to stop the quiver at the side of her mouth, she broke out into a laugh. "Pizza?" she asked between giggles.

"Yeah, sure."

Jed held the door open for her once they reached the truck.

Jillian grabbed the side of the door frame, but when she started to lift one leg to step up into the huge four-wheel-drive truck, she discovered the hard way that she had chosen the wrong skirt. She couldn't extend her legs wide enough apart to lift her foot onto the frame.

Trying to control her blush, and failing miserably, she backed up a step, glancing at Jed over her shoulder. "I can't get up. I think I should go change my skirt."

"No!" Jed exclaimed, then lowered his voice. "No," he said again, more calmly. "I'll boost you up. If you don't mind."

Not sure which would be more embarrassing, running into the house to change or having Jed help her up, Jillian nodded.

Without a word, Jed stood behind her and placed his hands on her hips, and with a little push, boosted her up enough to step into the truck. Before she knew it, Jed was already behind the wheel, the driver's door closed. "Ready?" he asked.

Jillian gulped, trying to ease the fluttering in her stomach. Stiffly, she nodded and fastened her seat belt with shaking hands. "Yes, let's go."

six

"So, how was your visit with your sister?"

Jillian dabbed the corner of her mouth with her napkin. "Very nice, thank you. I meet her at the mall every Sunday after church, and she always gets the gooiest and most fattening donut she can find because she doesn't have to share it with her kids."

"I think I can appreciate how she feels." Jed grinned.

"She's got four kids, and she needs the break."

Jed laughed. "Mark and Betsy are great kids, but some days I think if I hear one more round of 'Uncle Jed, Uncle Jed!' I'll scream."

Jillian nodded. "I know what you mean. After seeing other people's kids every day, sometimes I think I'd like to scream, too. But I wouldn't ever do anything else."

"So, does your sister go to the same church as you?"

Jillian wondered at his sudden change of subject, grateful for it at the same time. "No. She doesn't go to church at all."

Jed paused, a piece of pizza halfway to his mouth. He put it back on his plate and folded his hands on the table. "How long have you been a Christian, Jillian?"

"I guess about four years. How about you?"

"All my life."

She envied him. The routine, the stability, the bond of a family that loved God and loved each other was something she saw all the time but had never experienced. The faith his parents modeled and instilled in him as a child extended to the next generation, because she knew from Mark that his

68

whole family attended church regularly as well.

Likewise, Jed would probably marry a nice Christian woman and have nice Christian kids. She suddenly felt jealous of the unknown woman. "Must have been nice."

He smiled, his gaze becoming unfocused for a few seconds before he made eye contact with her again. She could only imagine the fond memories he held. In order for Jed to be baby-sitting and living with his sister's family, they no doubt had grown up very close.

"Yeah," he said, still smiling, "it was."

Soon only a few stray crumbs and one lone mushroom stem remained on the round tray. Jed paid the bill and led her outside. As Jed opened the passenger door, Jillian froze, having forgotten until this exact second her problem with her entrance into his truck. She eyed the step, knowing that again she would need Jed's help. She regretted her decision not to change her skirt when she had the chance.

Jed bowed. "Milady," he said a little too courteously as his head came up. He was obviously trying to stifle a smile. Without asking if she needed assistance, his hands grasped her firmly by the hips and he boosted her up once more. The touch was innocent enough, but it sent shivers through Jillian anyway.

They arrived at the theater in plenty of time. Jillian slithered down from the seat to the ground, the trip out much easier than the trip in.

Once inside, Jed followed Jillian instead of leading the way to the back, where he preferred to sit. Being so tall and broad-shouldered, he liked to be courteous to any unlucky short people who had the misfortune to get stuck sitting behind him. He said nothing, though, leaving the decision up to her.

Instead of scanning the theater, Jed watched Jillian nervously checking out the location of the empty seats, taking note of a few couples already starting to get cuddly in the back row. Her posture stiffened, she grabbed his hand, and then she led him to the back row. "I chose the back because you're so tall."

Jed pressed his lips together, but he couldn't help himself. "Was that an invitation or a warning?"

The way her eyebrows knotted and her lips tightened indicated that it was indeed a warning. He raised one hand in the air in his good-old-boy-scout routine. Not that he'd ever been a scout. "Your virtue is safe, milady."

"Don't push your luck, Jed."

He watched Jillian as she sank into her seat. She intrigued him. She fascinated him. She was intelligent and fun. To his surprise, she had encouraged him when he told her about his preparations for college next fall. Of course she had a higher education with her bachelor of music, so she knew the commitment involved, in addition to the expense of obtaining a degree.

True to his word, Jed behaved himself, enjoyed the movie, and kept his hands to himself. As the houselights came on, Jed wondered what he could do to further stretch out the evening. He slowly led her outside into the parking lot.

Jillian's voice broke his train of thought. "What are you grinning about?"

"I'm hungry."

"Hungry? After all that pizza?"

"I feel like a big sticky donut."

"You don't look like a big sticky donut."

"Aw, come on. Ever since you mentioned it when you were talking about your sister, I've been thinking of donuts."

Jillian opened her mouth to protest but changed her mind. Despite her intentions to tell him that they wouldn't be wise to see each other outside of their lessons, she didn't want the evening to end. Besides, one could never eat too many fattening donuts. Jillian rested her hands on the door frame of the truck, waiting for Jed to boost her up again, telling herself that next time they went out together, they would take her little car, and he could be the passenger.

She glanced over her shoulder, trying not to appear nervous as she watched him stuff his keys in his pocket. What was she doing making plans, even if they were only in her mind? Twice a week for piano lessons was enough.

Once inside, she fastened her seat belt, watching Jed easily swing himself into the truck and start the engine. She couldn't believe how effortlessly he had hoisted her up; she hadn't had time to make even a cursory hop. Jed had picked her up and placed her on the seat of the truck as if he were lifting a child.

His voice broke through her thoughts. "What are you staring at, Jillian? Do I have popcorn in my hair or something?"

She couldn't help her blush. "You lifted me so easily; it made me wonder if you worked out or something."

Jed chuckled. "Only on the job. Most of the tool caddies weigh more than you do."

Despite her best efforts to keep herself trim, Jillian knew she weighed a few pounds more than the books said she should, but she had no intention of telling that to Jed.

Unconsciously, Jillian pointed her finger to the right and inhaled to speak, but Jed shook his head. "This time I don't need directions. I know where the all-night donut shop is."

Immediately upon entering, they discovered a group of young men causing a ruckus in the corner, which was not the relaxing atmosphere they had hoped for.

With one hand on his arm, Jillian whispered as close as she could get to Jed's ear, "Let's bring a couple of donuts back to my place, and then I can make some decent coffee, too."

He leaned down and whispered his reply in her ear. "Only if you let me pay."

A deal she couldn't refuse.

She followed Jed to the counter to purchase their selections. When she reached for the napkins, the dispenser was empty. "I'll be right back; just get something chocolate for me," she said to Jed and walked to one of the tables to help herself. As she tugged a couple napkins out of the holder, conversation among the rowdy crowd in the corner stopped.

"Hey, babe, these ones are better."

Jillian raised her head to see everyone staring at her. Rather, they were staring down the neckline of her sweater as she leaned over, leering and making rude comments among themselves, loud enough so she could hear them, too. Standing abruptly, she pressed her hand to the neckline and turned toward Jed, who was busy talking to the clerk, laughing as he fished through his wallet. He wasn't looking in her direction.

As she turned her head forward again, two members of the obnoxious crowd left their table and approached her. She could smell the liquor on their breath from five feet away.

Jillian stepped backward, but found herself pressed against the wall. Since they were in a public establishment, she knew she probably wasn't in any real danger, but still, she didn't want to be humiliated if they tried to touch her.

Her attempt at confidence dissolved as the largest of the group continued to approach until he was within a foot of her. Jillian started to open her mouth to call out to Jed, but no sound came out. The stench of liquor nearly made her gag.

"Hey, babe, want some help?" he sneered. Her stomach churned.

From the counter, she heard Jed mumble something, and in a flash he stood beside her. "Let's get out of here." With his arm around her waist, he ushered her out as the onlookers watched in silence. As the door closed, the whistles, catcalls, and lewd remarks began.

Jed inserted the key into the lock on the passenger door. "I'm sorry, Jillian. I wasn't paying attention, and I should have been watching."

She rested one hand on his arm as he turned the key. "It's okay, Jed. It all happened so fast, and I really wasn't in any danger, even if they were a disgusting bunch."

Already standing beside her, Jed turned, then tipped her chin up with two fingers, positioning her so she was staring up into his face. In the glow of the distant streetlights, his blue eyes glistened, and his expression caused her heart to miss a beat.

"Jillian. . ." Jed's voice trailed off as his eyes closed and his head lowered. The butterfly touch of his lips on hers almost made Jillian sink to the ground as all the strength left her legs. When he pulled away, Jillian missed the brief contact; without thinking, she lifted her chin and leaned into him.

In response, Jed's hand moved from her chin to her nape, and his other hand, still holding the bag from the donut shop, brushed the small of her back. He tilted his head and kissed her fully on the mouth.

All coherent thought drifted out of Jillian's mind; the fact that they were standing outside in the parking lot registered, but barely, as she raised her arms to drape them around the back of his neck—and then she kissed him back. Jed's arms tightened around her as she rose on her toes and let herself drown in his kiss, until the sound of a car horn startled them apart.

Jillian backed up a step and stood frozen, unable to comprehend what she had just done. Jed backed up slowly, his eyes wide. Jillian wished she knew what he was thinking.

He stiffened, then opened the truck door. Jed reached inside, then turned back to her. "Donuts are in. You're next." As before, he lifted her with ease and gently guided her onto the seat.

Jillian cleared her throat, trying to appear calm, although inside, she was a bundle of nerves. "Am I being foolhardy inviting you over at this late hour?"

Jed started the engine, then turned to smile at her. "I don't think so."

His smile did funny things to her equilibrium. Feeling suddenly warm, Jillian started to roll the window down, thinking the fresh air would help her come to her senses. She looped her fingers over the window when it was three-quarters of the way down and inhaled deeply just as she heard the sound of footsteps.

"Hey, honey, where ya goin'?" the slurred voice of the guy from the donut shop drifted in. In the blink of an eye, his hand shot through the window and he grabbed her wrist before she realized what was happening. Jillian let out a startled squeak and tried to pull away, but he didn't let go.

In a flash, Jed's arm shot across her and grasped the drunk's wrist in an iron grip. He twisted until the man let go, but Jed didn't release him. Instead, he gave the man's wrist a few firm squeezes.

"That wasn't very nice," Jed growled. "Do you have something to say to the lady?"

The man cursed a blue streak and called Jillian a number of rude names. Jed increased the pressure and twisted again. "Well?" he snarled.

"Sorry! Ow! Sorry!"

Jed thrust the man's arm out the window. "You're lucky I'm in here and you're out there."

The drunk stumbled back into the donut shop. Jillian's heart pounded and her hands shook as she rubbed her wrist with her other hand. Shock started to take effect as the back of her eyes burned. She didn't want to cry, not here, not in front of Jed.

"You okay?" he asked. He reached one hand toward her, but Jillian automatically flinched, then regretted it. Jed leaned back in his seat and gripped the steering wheel with both hands.

Jillian nodded, not wanting to talk about it for fear of bursting into tears. "Let's just go home," she finally gulped.

Jed filled the entire trip home with light and cheerful conversation, helping Jillian put the unpleasant incident behind her.

She slid out of the truck one last time, her hand carefully clutching the hem of her skirt to protect her modesty. As she started to push the door shut, Jed caught it and pulled it open. "Wait," he mumbled.

Jillian's breath caught and her heartbeat quickened as Jed's hand moved toward her. He stepped beside her and started to bend down. Was he going to kiss her again? Jillian nearly melted at the thought. She started to move closer to him, but to her surprise, he didn't touch her. He reached past her, then leaned into the truck.

Grinning, he pulled out the bag of donuts from behind the seat and held them in the air. "Now, we can go in."

Jillian forced herself to smile. Was she doing the right thing?

seven

Without letting go of the bag of donuts, Jed toed off his cowboy boots, pushed them neatly in place on the shoe tray with his foot, then followed Jillian as she headed to the kitchen at the rear of the house, passing through the living room first.

By now, the living room was very familiar to him. Or at least, what should have been the living room. Converted to a serviceable music studio, it contained a shelf full of music books, a small couch for parents to sit and watch the lessons, Jillian's small chair, and taking up most of the room, the large shiny black grand piano. Since she only used the room for lessons, he wondered if they were going to stay in the kitchen with their coffee and donuts, rather than sit on the couch beside the piano. "I guess you never entertain in there," he commented on their way past.

Jillian turned her head slightly but did not stop walking. "No, the living room is for business only. The things people usually put in a living room are in the next biggest room, which really is the den. I have to make do with the rooms I have—it's not a large house."

Jed sat at the table and watched as she poured the water into the pot and then into the coffeemaker. The first time he met Jillian, he'd thought her beautiful. As the days and weeks went by, and the more he got to know her, the less he thought about it, although on days like today, her beauty nearly took his breath away.

Unlike Brenda, Jillian did not flaunt the beauty that God blessed her with. Quite the opposite, in fact. Until today, Jed had never seen her wearing makeup or flattering clothes.

He blinked twice, then wondered why in the world he thought of Brenda. Brenda no longer mattered to him. By moving in with his sister after losing his job, he'd managed to make a clean break and get on with his life. He had plans, and could see his future mapped out before him without looking back.

Jillian turned to face him. "There, the coffee's on. In a few minutes it will be ready, although I don't know why I'm making coffee at this hour."

Jed lifted his wrist to check the time. "If this was a weeknight, then it would be about time for my last coffee break. One cup of coffee won't keep me up. How about you?"

"One cup shouldn't bother me."

He started to reach for the bag of donuts, but something in Jillian's expression made him withdraw his hand and wait for her to speak. "You look like you're going to ask me something." He hoped it wasn't something he didn't want to hear.

"Jed, this has been on my mind all evening."

He forced a smile, his suspicions getting stronger. "Uh, yes?"

"About yesterday."

Now he knew he didn't want to hear it. Yesterday had been fun, but judging from Jillian's stiff posture and the firm set to her mouth, she wasn't about to discuss fun. "Why do I have the feeling that you're not going to tell me you're ready to try bungee jumping?"

"Jed, I'm really not the type to go jumping off swings in the middle of the night. I wanted to say I don't know what came over me, and that I'm not normally like that."

As far as he could recall, they'd had a lot of fun, even when she lost her shoe. "So I guess that means skydiving's out too." Not that he would ever try such a thing himself, but why was he disappointed?

"Jed, I'm trying to be serious."

"Well, skydiving may be a little extreme. Tennis?"

Her mouth opened, then shut, as if she changed her mind about what she was going to say. He hoped she wouldn't accuse him of trying to be dense on purpose, because that was exactly what he was trying to be.

Jed took advantage of her hesitation. "If I can't find my racket, I'm sure Liz has one I could borrow. I had to pick through my stuff carefully, so a lot of things are packed away in storage." He didn't care if he had to go buy another racket, maybe even two, one for Jillian as well, even though he knew he had to count every penny.

"Don't you think tennis is a summer sport? I can't see playing tennis wearing a coat. After all, it is winter."

"Oh. Right, I keep forgetting because there's no snow on the ground here. Well, I'll think of something else." He reached for the bag of donuts before she had a chance to respond. "Isn't that coffee ready yet?"

"I. . ." Her mouth snapped shut again. She turned to open a cupboard and reached for a pair of mugs.

Fortunately, she appeared to be in no rush as she poured the cream into a pretty little bowl with pink flowers on it, and set it beside a matching sugar bowl in the center of the table. He had the impression she had more to say, and that he'd like it even less than her denial she had enjoyed yesterday evening as much as he had. He tried to fight the premonition that a serious brush-off was coming. As much as he had neither the time nor the money to get involved in a relationship, he wanted to spend more time with Jillian.

She set everything on the table, then opened her mouth to speak again. Jed hastily opened the bag and stared inside. "Donut?" he asked, not giving her a chance to speak first.

Jillian sighed loudly, then turned to fetch some plates while Jed continued to stare at the donuts. He didn't want to hear what she had to say. Was she going to tell him to back off? Had he blown it by kissing her? He didn't move or raise his head, but he followed her with his eyes as she bent over and reached into the back of a cupboard for the napkins.

He still didn't know what had come over him, but when that drunk approached her inside the donut shop, he'd surprised himself with a surge of protectiveness. He'd had to kiss her afterward.

Why was he still looking at these stupid donuts? He didn't even want them. The only reason he suggested they buy some donuts was to extend the evening.

Jillian delicately placed two plates on the table, forcing him to look up. He handed her the bag of donuts he had been staring at for so long. "Here. You pick first."

In silence, she held the bag open, peeked in, then hesitated. "There's six in here. I thought you were only going to buy two."

He shrugged his shoulders, not sure of how to respond but not wanting to take his eyes off her. "I couldn't help myself. They all looked so good. I couldn't decide."

She picked out the smallest one and handed the bag back to him. "That's all I want. Take the rest home for your family. If you leave them here I'll eat them, and then I'll be sick."

Jed thought of offering to nurse her back to health but thought better of it. "Then I think I'll take the stickiest one now so the kids don't get it. Liz would kill me if she found chocolate fingerprints all over the place. She'd make me wipe down the walls."

"A woman after my own heart."

"Hmph. No comment."

She bit into the donut, sparing Jed from having to play any more verbal tag. "So, what church do you go to?" he asked. He wanted to learn everything he could about her.

For a second, she stopped chewing, then sipped her coffee and swallowed. "Huntington. It's across the street from the arena."

Jed closed one eye, trying to picture the area. Liz had told him a little about most of the churches in the area, so he knew about Huntington, but not much. "That's small, isn't it?"

She bit into the donut again and nodded. "How about you? I'll bet you go to that big one near the mall with Mark and the family."

"Yeah. I tag along with Liz's family on Sunday. So, you like it there? Do they have a ladies' Bible study once a week? I know you can't do anything in the evenings."

"No, they don't have anything like that there."

"I'll bet you play piano for them Sunday mornings, though."

"Actually, no, I don't."

"You don't? They have a whole band at my sister's church. I would think you could really get into that. They're all dedicated God-loving people, and they really know how to bring the congregation into a meaningful time of worship. And Doreen, the piano player, is going to be needing a replacement soon because she's really big and pregnant." Jed linked his fingers and held his arms in a circle in front of his stomach.

"Pardon me?"

"I should introduce you; you'd like her. Doreen and her husband, Edwin, are really into dogs, and he keeps telling everyone she's going to have a whole litter."

Jillian's mouth hung open, and Jed broke into a wide smile.

"Whenever he says that, she threatens to have him fixed, which always gives everyone a good laugh. The worship team is quite a lively bunch."

Jillian's face turned red. "Huntington's is small and quiet. The guitarist is good, but not outstanding."

"Why do you go to a small place like that?"

"The pastor preaches a good message, and there aren't any single men."

Their eyes met, and they finished their snack without further comment. Jed wasn't sure he wanted to know the reason behind that statement. The quiet, middle-of-the-night atmosphere of her kitchen was too intimate for such a discussion, especially after putting his foot in his mouth making that comment about Edwin and Doreen. He usually didn't babble, and his idiocy only proved how nervous he was.

Jillian delicately licked the tips of her fingers, doing funny things to Jed's insides. "This was a nice idea," she said quietly, then licked one finger again. "Thanks for the treat."

"You're welcome. And on that note, I should go. I have to get up early to get Mark off to school, and it's already well past midnight."

"How do you do it?"

"Do what?"

"Work so late every night and then get up early. When do you sleep?"

Jed felt his ears heat up. "I'll admit to the occasional afternoon nap after I get back from dropping Betsy off at school. But I still practice my piano lessons."

She smiled but didn't say anything, which was just as well.

"See you for lunch tomorrow, then?" Jed mumbled as he stepped into his cowboy boots. For a second, his heart clenched when he thought she was going to say no. He released his breath when she nodded and opened the door.

"Good night, Jillian." He leaned toward her, but she backed up a step. Jed didn't want to push his luck, so he nodded back and stepped outside.

"Good night, Jed. See you tomorrow."

Jed walked to his truck and started the ignition. He knew he wouldn't fall asleep quickly, and he knew it wouldn't be from too much caffeine.

ᵇ₠

Not being one to tempt fate, Jillian was ready and wearing a sweatshirt, jeans, and sneakers when Jed arrived to pick her up.

She never did figure out what went wrong, but the chance to tell him that she wouldn't be seeing him outside of lessons had never come up during their late-night conversation. Today would be different.

As she vaulted herself up into his truck, without his assistance this time, Jed started the conversation by teasing her about her jeans and the pink lace around the pockets. To top it off, when she complained and defended herself, he threatened to make her walk, then laughed at her when she became flustered. By the time they arrived at the local hamburger joint, she was laughing so hard she couldn't bring herself to spoil the mood.

Despite the questionable quality of the hamburger and fries and the bad coffee, Jillian couldn't remember the last time she had so much fun. They laughed and joked and teased each other throughout the entire meal, and stayed far longer than necessary in a fast-food establishment.

For some reason, she was hesitant to leave. To her dismay, especially since she didn't want to like him too much, Jillian discovered they shared much in common. Jillian had been fascinated, listening to Jed as he shared his funny stories. He ended with his dreams to study literature and his goals when he became a teacher.

Curiosity having got the better of her, she asked enough questions to find out what happened to make him move in with his sister. Apparently, he had been working at a good-paying job out of town, trying to put enough money aside for college, but he hadn't quite made enough when the mill closed. However, when he told her about the last few months at the mill, Jillian was left with the impression he purposely left something out, because at one point he became distant and evasive. Then he had changed the subject so fast she didn't know what hit her.

Before she knew it, Jed had jumped to his feet and pointed out the time, obviously worried that he would be late picking up his niece from kindergarten. Before she had time to think, he grabbed her hand and they dashed out the door, running hand in hand through the parking lot. He mimicked Betsy's reaction to seeing her Uncle Jed pick her up in the truck instead of walking, because he always walked, even in the rain. He described Betsy's own special umbrella with little yellow ducks wearing raincoats on it. Even though Jillian had never met Mark's little sister, she could picture her, cute as a button.

She stared at his taillights as he rounded the corner on his way to the school, wondering not only where the afternoon had gone but also how the opportunity never came up to have that serious little talk with him.

She inserted the key into the lock. Jed's next lesson wouldn't be until after Christmas; he'd had to cancel his Tuesday lesson because of something going on at the school. She found herself humming "Pop Goes the Weasel," then forced herself to switch to a Christmas carol.

ঌ

"Hi, Jed. You're right on time, as usual."

Jillian watched as Jed toed off his large cowboy boots and pushed them onto the mat with his foot. Trying to be discreet, she checked his boots as he hung his jacket on the coatrack, and bit back a smile when she noticed that the right boot had a prominent and permanent scuff mark on the back. As she did every lesson, Jillian sat in the chair beside the piano bench and smiled at him with her practiced teacher smile.

Jed turned to her with an animated grin. "I practiced, Miss Jefferson!"

Jillian wondered when he could possibly have found the time during the hectic holiday season, but she said nothing. Everything had been such a rush for her as well. She had delivered a small Christmas gift to all of her students, and as usual, some of them had given her small token gifts in return.

She had been surprised to receive two gifts from the Edwards household. Mark had given her a chocolate Santa, and Jed had given her a small Christmas tree ornament that played an electronic Christmas carol when a small button was pressed. She would never again hear "Silent Night" without thinking of him. But the tree was down now and the Christmas decorations all put away, and now lessons could start with renewed enthusiasm for the new year.

Just to see what kind of response he'd get, Jed raised his hands to the keyboard, smiled playfully at Jillian, and winked. He'd missed her. Even though he'd phoned a number of times, with all the rush and bustle of the Christmas season they never did have a chance to get together. And until today, when the kids had gone back to school, he'd had to stay home to baby-sit. But he'd had plenty of time to think about her.

"Jed, you're slouching. Holidays are over, and it's time to concentrate."

Jed grinned, straightened his back, and returned his thoughts to the music in front of him. Mark had been right. Mark warned him that "Miss Jefferson gets superstrict about sitting still after the holidays are over." Unlike Mark, though, he had no trouble settling down and keeping his feet on the floor.

"Come on now, Jed. Don't forget your proper hand position."

He tried not to laugh. He had no trouble with his hand position either. Most of the time he placed his hands wrong on purpose, just so she'd touch him. He noticed at some point she saw through him, and started to verbally remind him instead of actually repositioning his hands. She called it a "friendly reminder" when he playfully complained about her nagging.

He sucked in a deep breath to help focus his concentration. If he did these three songs to her satisfaction, including the dreaded "Pop Goes the Weasel," he would pass Book One. He had tried his best to practice with everyone home, but he'd had to battle Mark for the piano. The noise and activity nearly drove him to distraction. At least Betsy had been interested enough in a new video he had bought for her to let him practice uninterrupted for a while this morning.

He made a few mistakes on the first song, but she took him at his word that he had played it perfectly at home, and she passed him anyway. Of course, playing it by himself at home would never compare to the duet during lesson time. He always enjoyed the fancy stuff she played an octave lower to fill out the sound, once he got it right. She promised that one day he would be able to do the same.

Jed managed to play the second song without error, but Jillian still pointed out his uneven timing and a number of other inconsistencies, which he knew without her "friendly reminder."

He tried not to be disappointed. "Does this mean you're not going to pass me? It wasn't that bad, was it?" He wanted to pass Book One so bad he could barely sit still. He was so sick of the kiddy stuff; he wanted to play something good.

"Of course, it wasn't that bad, but I know you can do better. As an adult, my expectations are higher for you than the kids, even Mark. You have to remember that no matter how good you do at a song, you will never, ever, achieve perfection. There will always be something you feel you could have done better. Music is personal. No matter how near perfect you get it, every time you play it, it's different. Sometimes it changes with the mood you're in at the time. Am I making sense?"

Jed thought about it. Maybe he could see her point with the complicated stuff that Jillian played, but he didn't see how that affected "Pop Goes the Weasel." "I think so," he replied uncertainly. "I know I'm playing these kiddy songs different here than at home with Mark and Betsy running around screaming. At home I was annoyed and getting mad at them, and here I'm nervous."

Jillian crossed her arms and stared at him. "They're not 'kiddy' songs. They're 'beginner' songs. And what do you mean, I make you nervous?"

He grinned back. "I guess it's this thing I have from back in high school. Teachers are so intimidating."

"But you want to teach high school literature."

"And I should be good at it. I can be very intimidating too if I want to be."

Jillian stared blankly at him, and he couldn't even begin to guess her thoughts. "That's enough," she said. "Let's get back to the lesson. It's almost time for you to go, and I'm still waiting in anticipation to hear your favorite song."

He knew which one she was referring to without asking. Jed grimaced. "It's not my favorite song. And I don't have to worry about the time today. Betsy is going to a birthday party after school, and I don't have to pick her up. If you don't mind, I thought I'd stay for Mark's lesson."

First, she grinned, then her smile quickly dropped to a frown. "Good. Then you can see how well Mark behaves at his lesson. Often he runs here from school; I can tell because he's panting, but he won't admit it." She sat back in her chair, tapping her chin with her pencil, waiting for him to play.

He couldn't stall any longer. "Here we go," Jed said flatly, taking a deep breath as he positioned himself properly. " 'Pop Goes the Weasel,' the whole thing, adding the missing verse, playing by ear." He hesitated, then destroyed his proper posture by turning and sitting almost sideways on the bench to look at her. "You know, I've been humming this stupid thing all weekend, trying to figure out the whole song, so I hope you're satisfied with yourself." Without waiting for a reply, he turned back to the piano and repositioned himself in a huff.

Jillian tried unsuccessfully to repress a smile. "Temper, temper. Remember, the mood you're in affects the way you play the song."

"Then this weasel is going to really go 'pop,' " he grumbled under his breath, "and it will serve him right."

Jed prepared himself to start playing one more time, resigning himself to the fact that she really was going to make him play the silly song. He had the unwritten part all figured out and memorized at home, and now he would see how well he did under pressure, with Jillian sitting behind him, her arms crossed, listening and analyzing him.

Jillian listened to a meticulously played "Pop Goes the Weasel," the missing lines perfectly filled in. She really couldn't justify his constant complaining about it. She'd been humming it to herself all week, too.

"That was great, Jed! Now I'll play the accompaniment." As happened every time she played her part of the duet, her leg pressed up against his as they sat side by side on the bench. Even though this happened twice a week, she still found the sensation unnerving, not to mention distracting.

Together, they played the song again, Jillian following his lead, making a rousing musical "pop!" at the end of the song.

"Do I pass now?"

"You sure do."

Jed lifted both hands in the air in triumph. "Yippee! I've finished the kiddy songs!" He turned and gave Jillian such a heart-stopping smile, her breath caught. Slight crinkles at the corners of his gorgeous blue eyes emphasized how genuine his smile was. "So, what do I get for passing the book? You never gave me a single sticker. Mark shows me his stickers every week, you know."

"I don't know," Jillian gulped. "Suggest something."

Jed wiggled his eyebrows, only adding to the allure of his wide smile. "Dinner?"

"Dinner?" she echoed weakly.

His eyes twinkled. "Name the place. Your treat."

"*My* treat?" She wondered what she was getting suckered into. "I'll think about it."

The smile dropped to an exaggerated pout. "What do you mean, think about it? What do I get for passing?"

Jillian reached over and patted him on the head like a dog. "Congratulations, you pass. Good boy."

They both burst into peals of laughter, her hand still resting on the top of his head. His hair felt wonderfully thick and soft, and she twirled a few strands in her fingers, amazed at the feel of it. Wavy and untamed, the gentle shade of light brown blended perfectly with his clear blue eyes. Her fingers played with one of the flowing waves, which always seemed to have a mind of its own. No matter how she twisted it, it always sprang back to where it wanted to go. Strong and unfettered, it suited him.

Jed's eyes drifted shut, and he automatically leaned his head into her hand. As much as she liked to look into his dreamy blue eyes, with his eyes closed, Jed's expression became totally unguarded. The sweet half-smile on his face along with his unconscious sigh was Jillian's undoing.

She felt herself shudder as his hands slipped around her

waist. She closed her eyes and leaned into his solid chest as she continued to play with his hair.

At the same moment, they both opened their eyes and murmured each other's names. Her eyes drifted shut again as she welcomed his kiss. The part of her that warned her against becoming involved with Jed lost the battle as his kiss deepened and he stroked her back, sending hot shivers all the way through her.

Jed pulled away first, and Jillian immediately missed the contact. Rather than separate from him completely, she remained still, only inches from him.

When he kissed her again, Jillian melted completely into him. Her heart pounded as he showered her with countless short, gentle kisses.

"Eeewww! Gross! Uncle Jed! Miss Jefferson!"

Jillian and Jed bolted apart. Mark stood in the hall entrance, staring at them with his mouth hanging open.

Out of the corner of her eye, she saw Jed running his fingers through his hair to brush it back off his face. "Guess what, Mark?" Jillian noticed a quaver in Jed's voice as he spoke. "I passed Book One."

Jillian's brain refused to function, and words would not form. Her best student had just caught her sitting at the piano kissing his uncle Jed, and not just a peck on the cheek, either.

Mark didn't move. He clutched his book to his chest and stood stock-still, his eyes wide. "Well, forget it. If you ran out of stickers, you're not kissing me!"

Jillian was mortified. She couldn't think of a single thing to say.

Jed jumped to his feet. "It's okay, Mark. She only kissed me because I asked her to. Right, Miss Jefferson?"

Trying to regain her composure, she looked up at Jed. "Um, yes, Uncle Jed. That's right." She sucked in a deep breath and wished she could settle the frantic thumping of her heart. "Don't worry, Mark, I still have lots of stickers. Come on, have a seat and let's get started."

She couldn't face Jed as Mark sat on the bench, watching her out of the corner of his eye as he squirmed into position, apparently still not certain if he could trust her. Jillian tried to control the shaking of her hands as she smoothed her hair back, then settled into her own chair beside the piano bench. Jed sank down onto the couch reserved for parents who stayed to watch the lessons.

Coming down from the adrenaline rush, Jillian's knees trembled as she tried to concentrate on Mark and his piano lesson and not on his uncle Jed, who patiently listened as Mark diligently played the songs he had practiced so hard.

When she wasn't watching him, Jed watched Jillian as she struggled to maintain her dignity with Mark. However, he could tell by her shaking hands and slight tremble in her voice that she wasn't entirely successful.

If he could have, Jed would have kicked himself. What had happened? And why couldn't he laugh about it? Any other time, Mark's performance would have had him rolling in the aisles, but instead, his insides churned. Jillian was upset, and he was responsible. He knew how much her solid upright image meant to her, and knew he was on shaky ground as it was in his efforts to get closer to her.

If he were alone, he would have retired to a quiet place to pray for guidance. Since he couldn't, he did his best to calm his mind and ask God for help, and then, most of all, for wisdom.

Jillian pointed out a few more things for Mark to work on, then dismissed him. Her next student was waiting.

Jed wished he could say something before he left, but Mark already had left the piano. The next student was settling in, so Jed followed Mark to the shoe tray and stepped into his boots.

He tried to make eye contact, but Jillian avoided him.

Very politely, Mark opened the door in silence. "Come on, Uncle Jed," he said in a stage whisper, beckoning to him. "It's time to go!"

As Jed closed the door behind him, he finally met Jillian's eyes. She wasn't smiling.

eight

Jed walked home, his steps heavy, as Mark hopped along beside him, bouncing with his excitement over the new stickers in his book. Jed did not share his enthusiasm.

"See, Uncle Jed, I passed, and she didn't have to kiss me," Mark chattered. "And now you're all done with Book One! That's so totally radical, Uncle Jed! When we get home, I'll get Book Two out for you. There's way better songs in it. I'll show you the best ones, and show you my cheater notes. Just don't tell Miss Jefferson about them. And then we can. . ."

Jed did not feel very radical. He let Mark prattle on, barely paying attention to what the kid was saying. All Jed could think of was Jillian. He was falling hard and fast, despite his resolution to avoid getting involved in a relationship. Time and time again, Jillian proved she was nothing like Brenda. Jillian was in a class by herself. Professional, dignified, intelligent, and beautiful. And honest and unselfish. And from what he had seen so far, a dedicated Christian. No one could compare.

For himself, Jed didn't care that Mark saw them, or what Mark thought, but if Jillian cared, then it mattered. He wondered why it made such a difference; after all, Mark was his nephew, so it wasn't like Mark was just any student. But the fact that she was upset about it made the difference. What could he do? He'd have to have a talk with Mark, and then if he explained things to Jillian, maybe she'd feel better.

". . .and then you start to play some of that Bach and Beethoven stuff, and some of it is really neat, but some of it is really boring, but Miss Jefferson will tell you how good it is for you to play all that stuff and then she'll set that ticking thing and make you do it real fast, but then it really does start to sound good. And then in Book Four it gets even harder and she starts making you do scales with tons of black notes and. . ."

How could he convince Mark to keep this a secret? Like any typical eight-year-old boy, once you said the word *secret,* it became a general bulletin through the whole school population and entire neighborhood. Bribery? No, he would tell everyone the reason he got whatever he picked out. Threats? Another bad idea.

"Uncle Jed? Don't you want to hear about Book Four?"

Maybe the kid would forget all about it. Maybe it was already forgotten. He was constantly forgetting about his homework and making his bed. Kids forgot things all the time.

"Uncle Jed? Uncle Jed? Aren't you listening?"

"Huh? What, Mark? I'm sorry, I guess I didn't hear. What was that again?"

"I said, why didn't you just wait for her to get you a different sticker? Why did you let her kiss you? Gross!"

Maybe he wouldn't forget that quickly. "Mark, I asked her to kiss me."

"Eeww! Why? She's got great stickers. Girls got germs, you know. And cooties."

"I like to kiss Miss Jefferson." At Mark's horrified expression, Jed tried to scramble for another idea. "Doesn't your dad ever kiss your mom?"

"Oh. That. Yeah, he does."

"Well, it's kind of the same thing."

"Oh."

Jed could almost see it like a light going on inside Mark's

head. Finally, he was getting somewhere. "It's no big deal, Mark. Really. It's nothing."

"Oh. Okay."

Mark walked in silence the rest of the way home. Jed thought Mark looked very serious for a little kid. He was too young now, but in a couple of years he would start having girlfriends of his own. Jed prided himself on handling it so fast. Now he could get on with his bigger problem of convincing Jillian, which would be the hard part.

As soon as they entered the house, Jed hurried into the kitchen to start supper. Instead of going outside to play, Mark sat at the table and watched him. Jed thought his behavior unusual, but since he was starting a bit late, he didn't have time to concern himself. He had barely got everything going, his lunch packed, and was hurriedly trying to gulp down his coffee when Liz and Frank walked into the kitchen.

"Hi, Jed. How was your day?"

"Fine. Don't forget to pick Betsy up at 6:00; remember, today is Angela's birthday party. And I'm almost on my way." Jed grabbed his lunch pail and rushed to swallow the last gulp of his coffee before he dashed out the door.

Mark piped up. "Guess what, Mom, Dad?"

Frank and Liz started to peek inside the oven and pots on the stove. "What, Mark?" Frank asked absently.

"Uncle Jed and Miss Jefferson are getting married."

Jed choked on his coffee, spitting most of it into the sink, and dribbling some of it down the front of his shirt.

Liz dropped the pot lid and gasped. "Jed? Why didn't you tell me?" She stood straight and placed her hands on her hips, feet slightly apart. "Have I been missing something? Is there anything you want to tell me? Or do you have some explaining to do, little brother?"

Jed tried to speak through his cough, barely getting the

words out. "Mark! I'm not going to marry Miss Jefferson! What gave you an idea like that?" Jed wheezed for air as another fit of coughing seized him.

"You said it was just like Mom and Dad. And they have to because they're married."

Liz took advantage of Jed's inability to speak. "What do Mom and Dad have to do, Mark?"

Mark made a face. "You know! Kiss!" Mark opened his mouth and let his tongue hang out, grabbed his own neck with both hands as if choking himself, then crossed his eyes.

Jed's face burned as Liz and Frank stared at him. The tightening sensation in his throat wouldn't allow him to speak.

"I can hardly wait to hear this one," Liz said, crossing her arms and narrowing her eyes.

Mark continued on, unaware of Jed's predicament. "When I got to my piano lesson, Uncle Jed was kissing Miss Jefferson because he passed Book One. I told her she better not kiss me; I want stickers for passing. I know she's got a *huge* one of Mario and Luigi, but Uncle Jed said it was okay for her to kiss him because he asked her to. And it was just like you and Dad, you know, cause, like, you and Dad are married, and that's how babies are made, you know."

"Oh?" Liz looked down at Mark, then back at Jed, then pressed her lips tightly together. "Well, Uncle Jed? Want to tell me all about passing Book One?"

Thankfully, Frank had the sense to be quiet. Jed cleared his throat. "I'm going to be late for work!" he grumbled as he ran the dishcloth over the wet dribbles on the front of his shirt, then threw it in the sink. He made a grab for his lunch pail for the second time, and stormed out.

All the way to work, Jed's guts churned. If Liz and Frank hadn't guessed there was something happening between himself and Jillian before, they knew for sure now. But, worse than that, now Mark knew, and knew too much. Now the whole school, and probably every one of Jillian's students would hear about it. Jillian would be devastated.

Would Mark tell the whole school his uncle Jed was marrying his piano teacher? Or worse? Liz and Frank had better straighten the kid out about the reasons for kissing a girl. Although come to think of it, what were his reasons?

Jed ran in and punched his time card with only a minute to spare. He threw his stuff in his locker, changed into his work boots, and hurried to his station. Another night of the same old thing. Today he'd have to make an extra effort to keep his mind on his job.

❧

With relief, Jillian bade good-bye to the last student of the day. All evening, she hadn't been able to concentrate on anything except the heart-wrenching embarrassment of being interrupted by a child, a student no less, caught in the most exhilarating kiss of her entire lifetime, not that she'd been kissed that often. Now that she was finally alone, she could deal with it rationally. Her stomach flip-flopped thinking about it as she leaned with her back against the door.

Jillian covered her face with her hands and sagged into the door. She never did get around to telling Jed that she didn't think it wise to see him outside of piano lessons. And now this! No matter how much she liked him and enjoyed spending time with him, she wasn't going to risk her reputation or her heart for him. She had to come to a decision on which way she would proceed with Jed.

Her decision was redundant; either way, she lost. She could keep with her original plan to refuse to see him again except for piano lessons, but she didn't think she could handle the strain of seeing him twice a week and knowing there would be no more, now that she knew how much fun he was to be with. Her only other option would be to tell him to find another teacher, so she would never see him again. Jillian sank lower as she continued to lean against the door. She couldn't handle that, either.

She shuffled into the kitchen to make herself some tea to help her relax, but only stared into the bottom of the empty cup. She opened her Bible to read, but none of the words made sense. Instead of sitting up all night and moping, she decided to go to bed. She would be able to think more rationally in the morning.

Yawning as she hopped into bed, she switched off the light, but she found she couldn't close her eyes. Every time she did, all she could see was Jed with his eyes closed, his untamed hair falling onto his forehead and a lazy smile on his face. Either that or the horrified look on Mark Edwards' face as he stood in the entrance hall. She tried praying about it, begging God for answers, but she only came up with blanks.

At 2:07 A.M., Jillian turned to the clock radio for the hundredth time. Rather than stare at the ceiling all night unable to decide what to do, she shrugged on her housecoat and shuffled into the kitchen to make herself some chamomile tea in the hope that it would help her sleep.

Sitting at the table, she watched the kettle, waiting for it to boil. Outside, a rumbling sound echoed, then stopped in front of the house.

Jillian ran to the front window to peek through the blinds: Jed's truck. The interior light came on as the door opened. Jillian yanked her fingers out of the blinds and ran to the door, clutching the neckline of her housecoat to her throat when he knocked on the door. For a second, she considered leaving him standing outside, but she opened the door anyway.

A rush of cold air whooshed in as Jed stood in the doorway, staring at his feet. Splotches of dirt streaked his shirt, and his jeans were so ratty they had holes in them. His typically unruly hair lay flattened in places, and he smelled like a grease pit. The only clean part about him was his cowboy boots.

"What are you doing here? It's two in the morning!"

He shoved his hands in his pocket. "I know. I was on my way home from work and saw your kitchen light on. Can we talk?"

nine

Jed held his breath, hoping she wouldn't slam the door in his face.

"Now?" she asked. She stared up at him, eyes wide, her hands clutching desperately around the collar of her housecoat.

He studied the toes of his boots. "I had a feeling you wouldn't be able to sleep."

"Come in, Jed," she sighed, then stepped back to allow him entry. Jed closed the door behind himself, toed off his boots and kicked them onto the tray, then followed her into the kitchen, where the kettle whistled on the stove.

"Do you want some herbal tea? It's caffeine free."

All he could do was nod and watch as she busied herself making the tea. She looked cuddly and sweet in her baggy housecoat and bare feet. For the first time since he met her, her hair was a mess, but even still, she was the most beautiful woman he had ever known. Not only that, she wasn't making excuses for her appearance.

She turned her back to reach a couple of mugs in the cupboard. As she lifted her arms, the hem of her housecoat raised up, showing her cute little bare toes beneath it. His heart caught in his throat.

When she placed the steaming cup of tea in front of him, he took a slow sip, then swallowed it too quickly, scorching his throat, rather than spit it back into the cup. "This stuff tastes like boiled straw! How can you drink this?"

"It helps me sleep. And I like it."

Jed cradled the cup in his hands, painfully aware of Jillian staring at him as he took another cautious sip. He hoped the second sip wouldn't be as bad, but the strange taste of the tea made him grimace in distaste. He set the cup on the table, wondering how to refuse to drink any more without hurting Jillian's feelings.

As much as he needed to talk to her, now that she sat in front of him, staring at him, he couldn't think of a single thing to say. After a full shift, he was filthy, and since it had been a particularly busy night, he didn't smell too great, either. Jillian, on the other hand, looked great. Pleasantly mussed and bundled in a granny-style housecoat that was probably thicker than his overcoat, she still somehow managed to carry about her an air of dignity.

"Bunny slippers," he said as he leaned back in the chair. He folded his arms across his chest, trying to cover the coffee stain and other assorted splotches, although the condition of his clothing was the least of his worries.

"What?" Jillian started to raise her cup to her lips, then froze. "Bunny slippers? What are you talking about?"

"You need bunny slippers. They would suit you. You know, the kind with the floppy ears and big eyes that look up at you when you cross your ankles on the coffee table."

"I do not put my feet up on the coffee table."

"Well, then, you should start."

"Jed, it's two in the morning. I don't think you came here to discuss ridiculous footwear."

"No, I didn't." Jed stared into the half-empty cup, then sloshed the liquid around as he tried to think. "I know you were upset about Mark, uh, walking in on us like that."

Jillian didn't answer. Instead, she appeared to be paying too close attention to the pattern on her cup. She blinked a couple of times, and Jed's stomach tightened.

"He's just a kid," Jed blurted out. "And I had a little talk with him on the way home." And he had. He merely omitted telling her that things didn't exactly turn out the way he had planned. He hoped Liz and Frank had had a chance to have a better talk to Mark about kissing girls.

When she didn't respond, Jed reached across the table to touch her hand, but she pulled it away. His throat became so tight he wondered if he would be able to manage the words. "Do you want to pray about it? It always helps."

She clutched her cup again. "I don't think I'm ready to pray with you, Jed."

He knew exactly what she meant. He often participated in group prayer, praying for people he barely knew, if at all. This was different. This was personal. Intensely personal. Praying together with someone close lent itself to a certain intimacy, one he couldn't even begin to reason out. And in a group situation, the results of such prayers usually didn't directly affect him. This time, Jed not only wanted to pray for peace for Jillian, he needed to. The more he thought about it, the more important it became.

He also needed answers. He wanted to know why she resisted his efforts to draw her closer. He didn't think it was him in particular, but he couldn't be sure. While she didn't exactly push him away, she didn't encourage him either. But more than anything, while he was curious about why it bothered her so much, he wanted her to have some peace about the incident with Mark. From her reaction, and the fact that she was still bothered so much about it, he had a feeling things went far deeper than just a little embarrassment.

So, while Jillian stared into her cup, her eyes fixed on its contents, Jed lowered his head slightly, closed his eyes, and prayed alone.

When he opened his eyes, Jillian was still staring into her cup. The sight of her made him want to get up, pull her out of the chair, hold her tight, and kiss her again, if he didn't smell like lubricant and other assorted unmentionables.

She looked up at him, her eyes big and round. "What if word of this spreads to my other students?"

"So what if it does? You're entitled to a social life."

"But not at the piano, and not with a student's uncle."

Her words didn't bode well at all. "It'll be okay, Jillian, I promise."

She didn't answer. Instead she stood, hugged herself, then looked toward the door, then back at him. Jed decided he could take a hint, before he was asked to leave and never come back. He couldn't take that. "I guess I had better go; it's late."

He walked slowly to the door, listening to the shuffling sounds of Jillian behind him. She didn't say a word to him as he let himself out. He thought about turning around to say something, but the door closed as soon as he cleared the doorway, and the lock clicked as it engaged. He walked slowly to the truck, then tightly gripped the steering wheel for a few minutes before he started the engine.

It would be quite some time before he fell asleep tonight.

&

Jed and Betsy stood in the window and waved at Liz and Frank as they drove off to work. Again, Betsy woke far too early, especially after last night. Not only had he been extra late getting to bed, but he had also lain staring at the ceiling for hours. He was getting to know every bump and lump of stucco on a personal basis.

Jed yawned, making no effort to hide it from Betsy. "Hey, Pumpkin, I'll give you a nickel if you go wake Mark up. I'll give you two nickels if you do it without any yelling."

Betsy giggled. "You watch me, Uncle Jed!" She tiptoed down the hall, still giggling.

He smiled through another yawn. Betsy could be such a

good little girl when she wanted.

For a minute there was silence.

"You little monkey brain! Get outta here!"

Betsy shrieked and ran down the hall and jumped into Jed's arms, laughing wildly. "I didn't yell! I didn't yell!"

Jed closed his eyes, afraid to ask, but he had to know. "What did you do?" He remembered one morning from his youth when Liz had kept snapping the elastic on his underwear until he couldn't stand it. Did kids still do that to each other?

"I pulled his blankets off and tickled his feet. You owe me two nickels!"

He could live with that. "Tell you what. After Mark leaves for school, how about if we go to the mall and I'll let you spend those two nickels?"

"Oh, boy! Can I buy a new doll?"

It was a struggle, but he tried to look serious. "Not with two nickels. You're going to need more than that for a doll."

"Then I had better go get my bank!" Betsy jumped out of his arms and ran to her bedroom. Jed could hear the shaking and rattling of coins as she emptied the contents of her bank onto the floor.

Mark shuffled into the living room, rubbing his eyes. "I hate her. She's a brat."

"She's a little girl, and she's your sister." Now he knew how his parents felt, only in their case, Liz was the eldest, and she never let him forget it. But even though she was older, by the time he reached thirteen, he was taller. Much taller. And then he didn't let her forget it. At times, he pitied his parents.

"At least I don't have to kiss her."

Jed cringed. Obviously, Liz had not spoken to him like he'd hoped. He wanted to have another little talk with Mark about this kissing business, but this was not the opening he had planned.

"Then who would you want to kiss?"

Mark tilted his head, as if it would help him think better. "Well, Dad thinks that in a couple of years I might want to kiss Kimmy Albertson, but then Mom poked him and said for him not to give me any ideas."

"Do you like Kimmy?"

"Yeah, she's cool. She burps even better than Rodney."

Jed smiled. Nothing like true love. "Pretty cool for a girl, huh?"

"Yeah, for a girl."

"Come on, let's get you out the door on time."

Once Mark left for school, Jed stretched and decided to make a pot of coffee. He was going to need at least that to get him through the morning.

After sufficient coffee consumption, he helped Betsy tie her shoes as they prepared to go to the mall. Betsy could barely sit still, anticipating buying some new doll she had seen on television, which he hoped was not too expensive. He had a feeling this was going to be a costly trip.

"Got your seat belt on, Pumpkin? Let's go."

Betsy chattered all the way to the mall, going on and on about that doll. By the time they arrived, Jed was sick of hearing about it. He allowed her to pull him all the way to the toy department, skipping. Jed refused to skip, no matter how great this doll promised to be. Fortunately, the doll was not overpriced, so Jed bought it for her as a treat. He picked out a small model for Mark to be fair to both kids.

"Come on, Pumpkin, now it's time to buy what Uncle Jed came for. Want to help me pick the right color?"

"Yes! That'll be fun!"

"Hurry up, it's almost time to go back and get you to school. Want a hamburger for lunch?"

"Do I get the kids meal with the toy?"

❧

Jillian looked at the clock. She could almost hear Jed saying "Yup, time for me to go get Betsy"—except it was the wrong day.

How he got enough sleep to keep going was beyond her. Jillian couldn't survive on so little sleep from day to day, week after week. And yet, Jed had committed himself to this routine until next September, until he went to college, an entire year.

When Jed said he would do something, it was considered done. She envied his family. His commitment to them was not only commendable but done with such a spirit of love that Jillian was almost jealous of his sister.

Jed appeared happy and settled in his arrangement. She had met Liz once briefly when Mark started lessons a few years ago, and although Jed mentioned they were very much alike, she couldn't remember Liz. Jillian tried to imagine a feminine image of Jed but couldn't. As she stared off into space, she pictured Jed, his dazzling smile, his brilliant blue eyes, and his unruly brown hair, a lock of it constantly hanging in his face. Even without him there, she had to suppress an urge to push it back into place.

"Hi, Miss Jefferson. I practiced everything extra hard this week. Which one do you want to hear first?"

Jillian blinked, then tried to discreetly check the clock before focusing on her incoming student. She had to get her images of Jed out of her mind and get down to business.

"Good afternoon, Sheila. Pick whichever one you want first. Come and sit down and we'll get started."

❧

As the last student of the day left, Jillian locked the door, leaned her forehead into the back of the door, and yawned. She couldn't remember the last time she had been so tired.

With the events of yesterday, and then her very, very late night after Jed left, she felt ready to drop. She barely found the energy to make herself a peanut butter sandwich for dinner, spending the balance of the evening on autopilot before she crawled into bed.

Sometime in the middle of the night, she half woke to listen for a few seconds to what sounded like the low rumble of Jed's truck. Through the fog of interrupted sleep, she tried to work up the energy to peek out the window, but the sound faded and disappeared. She rolled over and went back to sleep and dreamed of Jed and sitting on the swing.

Sunlight was pouring in the window by the time Jillian awoke. After she dressed, Jillian put on a pot of coffee and stepped outside to retrieve the mail and newspaper. As she wrenched the paper out of the slot, a volume of flyers tumbled down around her feet. Grumbling about the volume of after-Christmas sale flyers, she bent to gather them. Sorting them with one hand, she reached up to the mailbox without looking.

Her hand jerked back when she came in contact with something fuzzy in the mailbox. A pair of bunny faces stared back at her. She pulled them out, but they weren't stuffed toys; they were slippers. She found a note attached.

> *Instructions—place one on each foot and position carefully on a solid coffee table. Improper usage voids warranty.*
>
> *Love, Jed*

Jillian stood on the doorstep, staring at the large blue faces, complete with big wide eyes, pink noses, and floppy ears. Bunny slippers? They looked ridiculous in her hand. Jillian couldn't begin to imagine how ludicrous they would look on her feet.

Jillian read the note again. Was this Jed's way of trying to cheer her up? She held the slippers at arm's length, and the utter silliness of the faces got the best of her, forcing her to grin. At the sound of a car going by, Jillian realized that she was still outside. Quick as a bunny, she backed up into the house and shut the door.

She stared at the note again, and her grin faded. *Love,* Jed? Did he sign all his little notes this way, or was the situation with him spiraling even more out of control? She hugged the slippers and walked into the kitchen. They were too cute to scuff along the floor.

Jillian placed them on the counter beside the coffeemaker, continuing to stare at them as she poured her coffee. The bunnies stared back.

She'd never seen anything so preposterous in her life. Bunny slippers. While she was sure, knowing Jed, he had meant to cheer her up, she couldn't imagine anyone giving her such an odd gift. In the past, when anyone, especially a man, gave her a gift it had always been something expensive, fancy, ultrafeminine, and with strings attached.

She dropped the bunny slippers on the floor, then slipped her feet into them. She shook her head, and shuffled over to the couch and as instructed, lifted her feet and rested them on the coffee table. The bunnies looked back at her, just like Jed said they would. They were absurd. Definitely undignified. And warm and fuzzy. And comfortable. Jillian wiggled her toes inside them and leaned back on the couch. She loved them.

Without getting up, she leaned over to the phone on the end table and dialed Jed's number.

A little girl answered. "Hello?"

"Hello, Betsy. Can I speak to Uncle Jed?"

"How did you know my name? Who is this?"

Jillian smiled at Betsy's plight, amused to be getting the

third degree from a little girl. "This is Miss Jefferson, the piano teacher. Your Uncle Jed told me your name. May I speak with him, please?"

"No, you can't."

Jillian's smile dropped at the thought of being screened without knowing why. "Why can't I speak to him, Betsy?"

" 'Cause he's having a shower. Wait. The water stopped." The phone crashed with a loud bang in Jillian's ear and Betsy screamed for Jed in the background. She listened to a series of loud thumps, as Betsy screamed to Jed that she had to tell him something.

Jillian's own face heated up and she considered hanging up rather than listen, when she heard Jed's voice in the distance. He gently admonished Betsy for calling him out of the shower unless it was an emergency. Jillian strained her ears to hear Betsy telling Jed it was the piano lady, who was still on the phone, waiting. Silence hung in the air.

"Hi, Jillian." Jed's embarrassment radiated over the phone. Jillian struggled to remember why she called in the first place.

Jillian looked down her legs at the bunnies, still resting on the coffee table, and wiggled them. "Thanks for the bunnies, Jed. They're adorable. This was so sweet. I don't know what to say."

He laughed in response. "You're welcome. Enjoy them. You'll have to model them for me."

"Anytime you want. But I should let you go. You're probably leaving a puddle on the rug."

Jed remained silent for a few seconds. "Oh, yeah. Kids, no tact. You busy this afternoon?"

"Uh, no, why do you ask?"

"How about modeling those slippers for me and then we could decide from there?"

"Well, I don't know."

"Come on, Jillian, I've got to see those slippers on you."

Jillian wiggled her feet, which were still on the coffee table, causing the bunny ears to flop. She grinned. "I guess so. Bye, Jed."

"Bye, Jillian."

Jillian smiled as she hung up the phone and wiggled her bunnies once again.

ten

Jillian answered the door, proudly wearing her new slippers. In response, Jed laughed when she pointedly looked down and wiggled her feet.

She looked up at him. "Here's Flopsy and Mopsy, but where's Cottontail and Peter?"

His wide smile nearly caused her to melt into a little puddle. "You have to model them on the coffee table, or remember, you void the warranty."

She couldn't imagine doing anything so horrible as to void the warranty. Jed stood before her with his arms crossed over his chest, waiting, but his playful smirk gave him away. After all his efforts to sneak them into her mailbox, she couldn't disappoint him.

Jillian led Jed through the house to the den, where she plopped herself down on the couch, leaned her head back, and carefully placed her feet, complete with bunnies, on the coffee table.

"There. Satisfied?"

"Satisfied. Let's go." Jed stood.

"Go?"

"I'm starving. Let's go grab some lunch. My treat."

Jillian stood, watching Jed as he started to walk to the front door. "But you didn't even give me a chance to properly thank you for the slippers."

"It's no big deal. You said thanks over the phone." Jed turned around completely to face her, resting both hands on his stomach. "Come on, I'm famished. Or do you want to wear those silly things out in public?"

Jillian's bunnied feet refused to move. That was it? He didn't expect anything in return for his gift? Not even a kiss? A choking feeling gripped her throat. No one had ever given her anything and not expected something in return. No one. She tried to fight the tears welling up in her eyes and failed.

"Jillian, what's wrong? Are you crying?" Jed stood before her in the blink of an eye. With one hand resting gently on her shoulder, he tenderly wiped a lone tear with the back of his finger as it slid down her cheek.

His gentle touch was her undoing. Her lower lip started to quiver and her eyes burned. Jillian buried her face in his chest, threw her arms around him, and let herself lose control. His arms tightened around her, making her sob harder.

Jed tightened his grip and stared down at the top of Jillian's head, completely at a loss to figure out what he'd said or done. They were only slippers, and they'd cost him less than an hour's wage. In fact, he thought he was being funny by slipping them into her mailbox in the middle of the night, only Jillian wasn't laughing. But she had been earlier. The last thing he wanted to do was upset her. The stupid slippers were meant to cheer her up, but apparently they'd had the opposite effect.

A warm spot seeped through his shirt, wet from her tears. Jillian's whole body shook as she continued to cry uncontrollably. Her muffled voice vibrated against his chest. "I'm so sorry, Jed. I feel like such a fool." Her hands released their grip around him, then she grabbed a handful of the front of his shirt and pressed her face into him again.

Unable to figure out what to say or do, Jed kept one arm around her back, and stroked her hair with the other. "Want to talk about it?"

She shook her head, still pressing her face against his shirt. "No, it's not important." Her whole body trembled as a new wet spot formed from yet another burst of tears.

"Jillian, if it upsets you this badly, I think it is important. Come on, you can tell me." Actually, he wasn't sure he wanted to know, because if it was this bad, he didn't know if he could deal with it, and he seriously doubted he could possibly be of any help. He took advantage of her inability to speak to pray for guidance and especially for wisdom. He seemed to be doing a lot of that lately.

Jillian sniffled and drew in a shuddering breath. Jed cringed as she readied herself to speak.

"This is the first time someone has ever given me a gift and not expected anything in return."

Her voice had been so soft and muffled that Jed barely heard what she said, but he had a nagging suspicion there was more to it than that. Gently, he continued to stroke her hair, waiting for her to continue.

"My parents split up when I was a kid. My mother's new husband and family always came first, and she didn't want us living with them, so Sue and I lived with our dad. Mother didn't visit often, but whenever Roger forced her to come, she always brought an outrageously expensive gift or a wonderful toy. She taunted me, usually in front of Roger's kids, to make me want whatever she brought real bad, and then she wouldn't give it to me until I gave her a big kiss and said 'I love you.' Then she'd gloat, her duty done, and we wouldn't see her for months."

Jed stroked her hair. "What about your dad? Didn't he do anything about that?"

"My father didn't want kids underfoot either. He was always so busy or out with different women, we hardly ever saw him, either. Sue and I were passed from sitter to sitter, and nanny to nanny. He gave us every toy imaginable just so we'd go away and leave him alone. I didn't want a room full of useless toys. I wanted my dad."

Jillian stopped to sniffle, then continued in a voice so soft he barely heard what she said. "The other kids were so jealous they wouldn't play with me, except when I got another new toy. I had to be satisfied with my music, and my sister."

Jed felt her trembling as another wet spot developed on his shirt with her muffled cries. As a child, his family had often done without, especially compared to some of the other kids in the neighborhood. But they'd been happy because God was in their midst.

Still stroking her hair, he tried to think of something that would help. "As a kid, that's gotta hurt. But surely there's been someone else that was special. A man?" Even though he knew she didn't have anyone to call her special at the moment, Jed thought a woman like Jillian would always have a lineup of suitors. Somehow, the thought irked him.

She sniffled again. "Every man I went out with made it very clear he wanted something for everything he did or gave to me. I seem to bring it out in them."

"You can't base all this on the experience of just a few jerks, Jillian."

She sniffled again, and her voice wavered as she spoke. "I was in love once, Jed, at least I thought I was. His name was Graham. He came from a nice stable home in a nice stable neighborhood, and went to a nice established church. I even thought we would get married. One day he told me he had something for me, and I thought it was an engagement ring. But it wasn't; it was a very flimsy negligee. He made his intentions very clear when he started undoing his shirt and insisting that he expected me to model it. I knew what he thought would happen next. And it didn't involve marriage or any commitment, at least on his part."

Jed couldn't think of a thing to say as he looked down at her tearstained face. The thought of a man trying to take advantage of Jillian made his blood boil. "What did you do?"

Jillian smiled weakly through her tears. "I didn't think I'd done anything to warrant that kind of suggestion. When I recovered from the shock, I ripped the negligee in half, then threw it back to him, box and all. Then I tried to leave. He was furious." She sniffled as her lip quivered. "He blocked the door and threatened me, so I ran into one of the bedrooms and locked the door. He started trying to break the door down, screaming vile things, what he was going to do with me when he got hold of me." She hugged herself, and her eyes temporarily became unfocused, staring at some unknown spot on the wall. She refocused and stared into space beyond Jed's shoulder, and her lower lip trembled again. "I was terrified, so I escaped out the window. I never saw him again."

"You jumped out a window?"

"It was ground level. Fortunately for me."

Jed drew her close once more, hugged her tight, rested his chin lightly on top of her head, and squeezed his eyes shut. Little snippets of conversation starting falling into place, things he hadn't understood at the time, but now he could. No wonder the incident with the drunk at the donut shop terrified her so much. His heart ached for her. He had no idea she carried such deep hurts on her shoulders, things he couldn't relate to after growing up in a very loving home. Sure, he'd done battle with Liz countless times, but that was only sibling rivalry, and never amounted to anything serious. They hadn't had much, as a family, but they had each other, and what was given was given freely.

"Jesus loves you, Jillian, and there are no strings attached."

"I know that, Jed, and you have no idea how much that gives me comfort; it's only been Him that's held me together. But, still, I'm not very good at dealing with people. And I know I'm not handling this very well. I don't know what to do, especially when you're being so. . ." she sniffled ". . .nice."

He had no idea what to say; all he could do was to trust that God would give him the right words. First John 4:15 came to mind, one of his favorite verses. "If anyone acknowledges that Jesus is the Son of God, God lives in him and he in God." It was so simple, yet so powerful. "God loves you, Jillian. He's given you salvation through Jesus Christ, and all the love that goes with His Son. It's a gift. All you have to do is take it."

Jillian sniffled and nodded her head against his chest. "I know. It took me a while to accept that, but I have. I guess there's just still. . .scars on my heart. Thank you, Jed," she whimpered.

They stood in silence, allowing Jed to give Jillian the time she needed to calm herself. He was positive that so many things in his own life were gifts from God, including the developing friendship with Jillian. In addition to being better able to understand her, he could see this was a good release for her. While not exactly fun, this conversation was necessary for both of them.

Jillian sniffled and pushed herself away from him. "I'm so sorry, Jed. You said you were starving. Would you like to go out for something to eat?"

Jed touched the wet splotches on his shirt. He wasn't about to go out in public like this. Jillian didn't look too great herself, with her puffy red eyes, tearstained face, and shiny nose. "I have a better idea. Want to stay here and just have a sandwich or something fast?"

Jillian swiped at her eyes with the back of her hand. "Maybe we should. I probably look terrible, don't I? I'm so sorry for falling apart on you like this." She sniffled again.

Jed touched her cheek with his fingertips. "Don't be. It probably feels good to get it off your chest, doesn't it?"

"Yes, in a way, it does. Thank you, Jed." Jillian kept her eyes averted, and her eyes settled on the blotches her tears had left on his shirt. "I think I made a mess on your shirt. I'm so sorry. That might stain. I should wash it."

Jed was not about to start undressing in front of Jillian, especially after hearing her story about the negligee. He covered one of the wet spots with his hand. "Don't worry about it. I'll just keep my jacket done up when I go get Betsy. I have to change into a different shirt for work, anyway. Either that, or if you splash some old coffee down the front of me, no one will know the difference." He forced himself to give her his Boy-Scout smile, even though he really wasn't in a teasing mood.

She swiped at her eyes with her forearm and cleared her throat. "Excuse me, I'll see what we can come up with for lunch."

Jed's stomach grumbled at the mere mention of food. He followed Jillian into the kitchen, then watched helplessly as she rummaged through the fridge, despite his offer to help. As she fussed about the kitchen, he tried to imagine what it would be like to grow up so lonely and neglected. He could also understand her apparent unwillingness to trust him. The biggest problem was, he wondered what he could do about it.

His parents were still happily married, and he phoned or visited them whenever he could. Throughout his childhood years, there never seemed to be money for extras, but they certainly never did without anything they needed. As a family, they enjoyed their time together, participating in a variety of activities, both in and out of church. Above all, his parents, through love and by example, imparted to him the love of God in his life. For that, Jed would be eternally grateful.

From what Jillian had said, it seemed she had enjoyed none of the same privileges, and his heart ached for her. He knew she was close to her sister, but they seemed to be drawn together by bad circumstances as much as anything else. He wondered at what point she had learned to trust in God, although it really didn't matter. The fact that she knew God's love and depended on Him now was what counted.

Lunch conversation stayed at a minimum, centering around small talk, and Jed didn't try to steer the conversation deeper; he wanted to give Jillian the time she needed to recover from her crying jag. As well, he also needed time to digest everything he had learned.

By the time they finished, only fifteen minutes remained before Jed had to leave to pick Betsy up from the school. Despite Jillian's protests, he insisted on helping clean up and wash dishes. The whole time they worked together, Jillian deliberately avoided eye contact.

The sensible part of him said this would be a good time to back off. He had plans for his future, and they didn't include a woman with extra baggage to carry. She couldn't have made more clear that she wanted to keep him at arm's distance, but when push came to shove, she wasn't exactly telling him to go away. Jillian had enough problems of her own, and as far as Jed could see, she didn't know what she wanted herself, beyond her career. But Jed knew what he wanted, didn't he? And that was paving his road to college with no distractions. Wasn't it?

He washed the last dish and drained the sink, then watched Jillian. She still fought the odd sniffle as she put everything away in silence. His grand plans for the future might be modified, but he realized that for the moment, he had only one goal in mind.

Jed stopped Jillian as she stacked the last plate in the cupboard. "You know what I want to do right now?" he asked.

Like a frightened doe, she turned her face to look over her shoulder, her big round eyes still red and puffy from crying.

His heart clenched, and he reached to her waist, turned her so that she faced him, and pulled her into him, pressing them together from head to toe. He tilted his head and leaned his cheek onto the top of her head. "To hold you," he murmured into her hair.

Jillian leaned into him, enjoying the comfort of Jed's touch. Another rush of confusion washed through her as his arms wrapped around her. "Watch it. If you're not careful, you might get another wet spot on your shirt."

He nestled his face into her hair. "I'll take my chances."

The press of tears no longer threatened Jillian, now that she was nestled safely in the comfort of Jed's arms. She cherished the support he offered for the moment, and refused to think about tomorrow, after he had time to think things through.

His voice rumbled in his chest as he spoke. "It's time for me to go get Betsy." She inhaled deeply, taking in the faint scent of fabric softener along with the stronger fragrance of his aftershave before they separated.

As he walked away, Jillian wondered if he would ever come back.

❧

Immediately upon awakening, Jillian dangled her legs off the bed and tucked her feet into her new bunny slippers.

Instead of concentrating on her itinerary, after she got dressed she shuffled into the den and sat on the couch, her ankles crossed on the coffee table, and stared at the bunnies on her feet. If the silly things weren't so large, she would have been tempted to sleep with them on. Jillian wondered if she was losing it, because she had never been sentimental in her life. Not only that, but the ludicrous slippers destroyed the dignified image she had worked so hard for. Strangely enough, she didn't care if any of her neighbors saw her. The bunnies were a gift from Jed.

Today was Friday, and all she could think about was Jed's piano lesson. After her overly sensitive reaction to his simple gift, she doubted he would come. The more the day wore on, the more agitated she became. At the sound of a knock on the door, the pile of music books in her hand hit the floor, scattering around her. She ran to the door, nearly tripping on the bunnies.

Drawing a deep breath, Jillian opened the door. "Hi, Jed. You're a bit early." Jillian was grateful he was. A few minutes more, and she would have driven herself completely insane.

"Hi." His gaze dropped to her feet. "Blue is your color, I think."

All she could do was smile weakly up at him, her heart in her throat. Jed's brilliant white smile quickened her heartbeat, leaving her light-headed. She stepped back to let him in, because she could no longer stand still.

"Want to know why I'm so early?"

Her feet froze and her hands started to tremble. Half the night and all day, she had agonized over his reaction to her uncontrolled outburst, and she dreaded his decision after he had time to think about it. But if he chose to keep his distance after witnessing her unstable reaction to an innocent gift, wasn't that what she wanted all along? If so, then why did she feel so heavyhearted? It terrified her to think he would quit lessons.

"You promised me something."

Jillian tried to think as she stared blankly at him. Her mind zinged in a million directions that had nothing to do with promises.

"I'll give you a hint. I passed Book One."

Book One. Jillian struggled to remember that far back. The day he passed Book One he had played "Pop Goes the Weasel." He had been a bit testy at first, but as he played it, he loosened up, and after that he had kissed her. She didn't dare guess what he was thinking.

"You said you'd take me out to dinner."

"Dinner," she echoed.

He grinned as if he didn't have a care in the world. Jillian thought she could have hugged him, but she didn't dare touch him.

"When?" she asked weakly.

"Saturday. Do I get to pick where?" He raised his eyebrows.

All she could do was nod.

He shook his head. "No. You choose. Not only do you know the better places; you're paying."

She already felt like her head was spinning without the added verbal runaround. "Then why did you ask if you got to pick?"

"Just testing." He shrugged his shoulders.

Her mind went blank. She couldn't have thought of a response if her life depended on it. "I think we should start your lesson. I'll decide where we're going later."

Jillian tried very hard to concentrate on the lesson, but she couldn't. After everything that had happened with Jed, she had too many things to consider. Already, they were running behind, but Jed was one student she couldn't let go overtime, because he had to leave on time to pick up Betsy no matter what. She focused on a section Jed found difficult, and made an attempt to encourage him to try harder.

Jed tried very hard to concentrate on the lesson, but he couldn't. He could only concentrate on Jillian. She was obviously still rattled, even though he had tried his best to keep conversation light. However, she wasn't as focused as usual. He'd even managed to tease her, but it didn't work. She spoke too quickly, her movements were too jerky, and her piano playing too mechanical. He iistened as she attempted to explain what he was doing wrong, but her instructions went in one ear and out the other.

What was happening? All he had wanted to do was take piano lessons. When had that changed? Once he finally got up the nerve to ask her out, separate from lesson time, he was glad he did, because they had a lot of fun together. After the incident at the donut shop, not only did he feel he had to protect her, he wanted to, even needed to. Beyond becoming protective, he'd become territorial, and that wasn't good. Then he'd kissed her. As if things weren't complicated enough, she willingly kissed him back. Both times. And he wanted to do it again, and again.

Jed blinked hard, then shook his head in an attempt to return his concentration to his lesson.

As she tried to think of another way to explain something he wasn't understanding, she licked her lips, and Jed's brain froze. He stared at her mouth, and his thoughts wandered again to the way he kissed her on their last lesson, which had been great, until Mark interrupted. Her vulnerability and openness about what troubled her drew him all the more.

"Jed, are you listening to me?"

He blinked and forced himself to smile. "Yeah, sure. I was just thinking. What did you say again?"

"I give up. I think we're done, anyway."

Jed focused on her face, first on her wide green eyes, then on her full lips. She must have known what he was thinking about, because she inhaled suddenly, then touched her fingertips to her bottom lip.

Unable to resist, Jed lightly grasped her hand, pulled it down, then ran the fingers of his other hand lightly over her bottom lip. Her eyes widened, but she didn't shy away. It was all the encouragement he needed. He whispered her name, pressed his thumb gently into her soft lower lip, brushed his fingers down to her chin, and kissed her.

A beeping sound forced them to separate.

Jillian stared at him, her face red, her unsteady breathing doing strange things to Jed's thinking processes. "What is that?" Jillian asked. "Do you have a pager or something?"

Jed blushed. "I set the alarm on my watch. Just in case I lost track of the time."

"Betsy," she said weakly.

"I don't want to phone and disturb your lessons tomorrow, so can you tell me now how I should dress for dinner?"

"I haven't decided yet, but no jeans, and wear a tie."

"Suit jacket?"

"Do you own one?"

"Believe it or not, I do." He grinned.

"Well. . ." Jillian tilted her head and held one finger to her chin. It only increased Jed's desire to kiss her. "If you want, but it's not necessary. I don't want to go anywhere so exclusive that you would feel embarrassed if I paid the bill."

He'd never considered if he would feel awkward about a woman paying the bill in a restaurant, because it had never happened before. "Don't worry about it. I think I can handle it."

"You'd better go. I'll see you tomorrow, Jed."

He could hardly wait.

eleven

The doorbell chimed as Jillian completed the final touches on her hair. Instead of merely curling it, she had swept it up for a more sophisticated image. After one final glimpse of herself in the mirror, she hurried down the stairs.

When she opened the door, her breath caught. Beneath his open coat, Jed wore a dark dinner jacket, accompanied by a crisp white shirt and silk tie. His flawlessly pressed slacks fit him perfectly, and for a final touch, polished black shoes replaced his usual scuffed cowboy boots.

Her eyes traveled back up his tall frame, taking in every detail until she gazed into his face. Clean shaven and sporting a recent haircut, he looked immaculate, even respectable, except for the Mickey Mouse on his tie. His grin made her foolish heart flutter.

"Wow," she exclaimed softly. "Little Jed?"

Jed studied Jillian with an appreciative stare, not so sure this was such a good idea, after all. He recalled the first time they met, his first impression of her, and how different she looked now. His heart slammed in his chest as he tried to take in everything at once.

While not revealing, the soft fabric of her dress flowed over every curve, accenting her hourglass figure. With her hair swept up in some kind of wavy style that begged a man's touch, it was all he could do to keep his hands at his sides.

How did she expect him to take her out for dinner with her looking like that? He could barely breathe, never mind function like a human being.

"Wow," he echoed playfully, struggling to keep the rasp out of his voice. "Miss Jefferson. You look good enough to eat." Her gorgeous green eyes widened as Jed realized what he just said. He looked pointedly away from her and pulled at his collar to ease the choking sensation in his throat. "Shall we go?"

She nodded, then tilted her head with a slight motion to the side. "I have to check and make sure the back door is locked. I'll be right back."

Jed watched her from behind as she turned and walked down the hall, appreciating every feminine movement. Upon her return, he held her coat for her as she slipped it on, then he let her rest her tiny hand on his arm as she stepped into a pair of high-heeled shoes the same color as her dress. He knew she didn't try, but she would turn the head of every man in the vicinity. His breath caught when she smiled up at him. He hoped he would live through the evening without a heart failure.

"Jed? Are you feeling okay? Your face is flushed. If you're not feeling well, we can do this another day."

Not on his life. Jed let his breath out in a whoosh of air, not realizing he had been holding it. "I'm okay, just got a tickle in my throat." He pressed his fist into the center of his chest and made a small cough to clear his constricted airways before he choked. "So, where are we going? Do I need directions?"

Jillian gave him a backward glance as she locked the front door on the way out. "Downtown. We're going to the new revolving restaurant. You keep mentioning bungee jumping, so I'm assuming you're not afraid of heights. It will also give you a good view of the skyline. I timed our reservation so we can enjoy the sunset."

Trying to be the perfect gentleman, Jed helped her up into his truck as delicately as possible. "Sounds good." From what he heard, being at The Loft would make it hard on his male pride if she paid the bill there, but he had been adequately forewarned. But truthfully, he'd only been teasing Jillian about treating him. He would be the one paying—not that she couldn't afford it. Come to think of it, knowing what she charged for lessons, if she ever chose to expand into full-time hours, she would be making much more than he would as a high school teacher, even after he earned his degree. In the back of his mind, he asked himself why he would care.

The breathtaking ride up the glass elevator on the outside of the building provided them with a magnificent view of the city as they quickly rose above the height of the surrounding buildings. Once inside, the hostess seated them at a window table.

The city stretched out below them. With the sun almost set, the horizon glowed in hues of bright pink and vivid purples. Tall downtown skyscrapers dotted with lights were majestically silhouetted against the skyline. The head waiter informed them the restaurant would make approximately one full revolution in the time it would take to finish dinner.

Jed gazed out the window. "I've never been on one of these things before. I know it's moving, but you really can't tell unless you look real closely at the table and the window frame. I wonder how fast we're turning."

Jillian had no idea. Dressed in well-fitting jeans and the usual cotton shirt, Jed normally would turn any female head, but dressed to the nines as he was today, he made her head spin, without the additional movement of the restaurant. She felt like a lovesick puppy, gazing starry-eyed at him across the table. Just because he didn't discard her after her emotional outburst was no reason to idolize the man, but she couldn't help but continue to stare, starstruck, at him.

He seemed not to notice. All his attention was focused outside the large windows. "This is quite the bird's-eye view from here. I wonder if we'll be able to see Liz's house." He turned and grinned at her. Jillian's heart skipped a beat. "Or your house."

Before she could reply, the waiter returned to inquire about bar selections and present them with their menus, allowing Jillian time to compose herself. They both ordered coffee to start, and the waiter left.

She reached across the table, brushing her fingers against his arm as she spoke. "Order whatever you want, Jed. This is my treat, and the sky's the limit. You deserve it. I've never heard 'Pop Goes the Weasel' done so well in my life."

Jed grunted. "Come on now, Jillian, I feel silly playing all that kiddy stuff. And you're going to be sorry you said that. What if I ordered the most expensive thing on the menu? You're going to wish you had simply given me a sticker."

She laid her menu flat on the table. "Don't feel silly; everyone has to start somewhere. It's not so simple when you're first learning. I played all that kiddy stuff too, you know."

"I know you did," he grumbled, "but when you did it you were probably eight years old. I'm a little older than that."

"I was six. As you can probably guess, I poured my heart and soul into the piano as a child. And that's beside the point. If it's any consolation, I admire you for starting now, as an adult. You've got guts. I hope you stick with it."

Jed turned his head to look out the window. "What every man wants to hear from a woman," he mumbled. "He's got guts."

Just like a little boy who didn't like being told he couldn't have a cookie before dinner, Jed's head lowered, and his lower lip stuck out. In all his masculine attire, Mickey Mouse tie aside, Jed's image presented quite a contrasting picture to his little-boy pout. Jillian bit her lower lip, but failed to control her laughter. First, she giggled, sputtering to hold back, then she covered her mouth with both hands. In the end, she burst into laughter, anyway. At that moment the waiter arrived to take their orders, giving her time to collect herself.

Resting her finger on the menu, she gave the waiter her order between giggles, then watched him write down both orders. When he left, Jed was staring at her.

"I love to watch you laugh. You know, you're as pretty as your name."

She couldn't help it. She blushed.

"Your name is so delightful. Jillian Jefferson. It suits you. What's your middle name?"

Jillian's cheeks heated up even more. "It's silly. Forget it."

"No, come on, tell me."

"June. My full name is Jillian June Jefferson."

"Alliteration. Effective. And beautiful."

Jillian's mouth gaped. She ignored the "beautiful" comment—but alliteration? She hadn't heard the term since high school. Up until now, she couldn't imagine Jed teaching high school literature. Maybe it wasn't so far off after all. "Well, what's your middle name? And I'll bet Jed is short for Jedediah."

He sighed and closed his eyes. "Jedediah. Beloved of the Lord."

"Come on, Jed, your middle name. I told you mine, so you can tell me yours."

"Ezekiel," he mumbled. "It means strength of God. My mother really did her homework."

Jillian snickered. Jed shrunk in his chair. "Jedediah Ezekiel Davies. Your initials are J.E.D., the name Jed. I like it."

"My mother thought it was cute." He sneered on the word "cute."

"Yes, it is cute." Jillian tried not to giggle again, but failed. "It suits you."

Jed straightened, sitting tall in the chair, emphasizing his size and the masculine width of his shoulders. "Get serious. Do I look 'cute' to you?"

All she could do was stare. He was a long way past cute.

Jed lowered his head. "Let's change the subject," he mumbled.

Her eyes softened, then became misty. "You're a nice man, Jedediah Ezekiel Davies."

Fortunately, their dinners arrived, sparing him the need for a response. The only time anyone ever used his horrible name was when his mother was furious at something really stupid he'd done, but when Jillian said it in that honey sweet voice, it was different. Her words and tone rushed over him, piercing him all the way to his soul. And his heart.

Jed said a short prayer of thanks over their meal. By the time they finished dinner and dessert, they had indeed made one complete revolution, just as the waiter promised.

When the bill came, Jillian scooped it up before he had the chance to touch it. Before he could protest, Jillian silenced him with a look that would have stopped a herd of wild elephants, then smiled sweetly at the waiter and handed him her credit card.

She turned to him when the waiter left. "I told you this was my treat, Jed. You deserve it. Now, don't insult me by trying to be gallant."

Jed tried to smile and hoped it didn't look as phony as it felt. He really hadn't been serious, nor had he thought she would take him seriously. "Next weekend, will you let me take you out and it'll be my treat?"

She shook her head. "No. I didn't do this to take turns. I wanted to treat you because you deserve it for all your hard work. Now be quiet and quit complaining."

Jed tried to appear casual on the outside, but inside, he was all choked up. Of course, it was only dinner, but this was the first time a woman had ever treated him to anything other than small birthday gifts. Brenda certainly never had.

At the time, he thought he'd fallen in love, and he thought Brenda loved him back. At first, they'd had fun together, and he gladly shared everything he had with her. Before long, she started asking for things, small things, then more expensive items she claimed to need, and then later, she claimed to be desperate and asked him for what she called a small loan, just for a few months. Since he was saving for college, however, the loan had not been small for him.

The next day he stopped by Brenda's house after work to discover Brenda and everything she owned—and everything of his she'd borrowed—were gone. Even though she'd asked for it, he hadn't given her the key to his condo, and he was glad now he hadn't, or else she would have cleaned that out, too. He hadn't been able to find her. No one, not even her parents, knew where she went, but her neighbor, a supposed friend of hers, a man, mysteriously packed up and moved out the same day.

She'd said she loved him, and he'd believed her. From that day on, he swore he'd never allow himself to be used like that again. She had bled him dry from both his heart and his bankbook, at the same time, forcing him to postpone his dream of a college education. The next day, he'd been told the plant was closing, and as corporate secretary, Brenda would have known that beforehand. Half the town, himself included, was suddenly unemployed. Through God's grace, he found another job quickly, except he had to sell his condo and move quickly. If it wasn't for Liz's needing a sitter, he could never have saved enough money for college while paying for a place to stay in Vancouver, where accommodation was far more expensive.

The waiter returned with Jillian's credit card and the receipt for her signature. Jed couldn't help but stare as she tucked it into her wallet, then back into her purse.

Jed was flabbergasted. What he felt for Brenda could in no way compare to how he felt about Jillian; he really hadn't been in love at all, he realized now. Friends, yes, and she'd played on his sympathies and tugged on his heartstrings to get what she wanted. But that was all. His feelings for Brenda were nothing like what he felt now for Jillian.

All his defenses came crashing down as Jillian smoothed her skirt, then folded her hands on the table, and smiled sweetly. His throat constricted. His last excuse was gone. He had no choice left but to admit to himself he was helplessly and hopelessly in love with Jillian Jefferson, the piano teacher.

"Ready to go?" she asked, completely unaware of the confused state of his heart. Jed stood and escorted her to the elevator door.

"How would you like to go up a floor and walk around the observation deck?" Jed asked as they waited for the elevator. He needed time to think. He couldn't let the evening end yet.

Jillian smiled and pressed the "up" button.

When the elevator door swooshed shut behind them as they entered the observation level, Jed gently grasped Jillian's hand. She didn't pull away, so he slowly led her around the perimeter, gazing out the window at the bright lights of the city shining below.

Alone in the semidarkness of the observation deck, talk was unnecessary, allowing Jed to enjoy Jillian's company in silence. They walked slowly, hand in hand, looking out the window of the observation room. No noise disturbed them, no appointments loomed, no schedules needed to be met. Except for the slight drone of the restaurant under them, they could have been alone in the universe, the city lights stretched out beneath them, miniature cars inching their silent way on the streets far below.

Jillian stopped to point out a few of the older landmark buildings in the area. When she leaned on the rail, then touched her finger to the glass, Jed slipped his hands around her waist. She didn't protest. He wanted to never let her go. She slid within the circle of his hands until she faced him, then rested her palms on his chest, keeping them a respectable distance apart. Jed didn't feel like being respectable.

His voice came out much lower pitched than it should have. "Is this where I'm supposed to thank you for a lovely evening, or do I wait until we get home? I've never had a woman take me out before, and I'm not sure what to do." He forced himself to smile. "And I'd like to know what you're going to do to top this when I pass Book Two."

Jillian's voice also came out soft and husky, doing more strange things to his insides. "I don't know. We've barely started."

His fingers found their way into her hair. "That's true, we haven't really." Jed couldn't believe the direction of their conversation. The lesson book was the furthest thing from his mind. The thing foremost in his thoughts was Jillian's sweetness, the silky feel of her hair, and the slight herbal fragrance of her shampoo. As he ran his fingers over the silken strands, Jillian's eyes drifted shut, and before he could talk himself out of it, Jed closed his eyes, lowered his head, and kissed her. When her arms floated up around his neck, Jed wondered if he'd died and gone to heaven. In the background, soft music played, adding to the atmosphere of romance.

He'd never been the romantic type, but Jed couldn't stop his emotions from spiraling out of control. Before someone walked in on them, Jed reluctantly ended the kiss, but rather than let the moment end, he held her tight. She fit just right in his arms, her head neatly tucked beneath his chin. Deep in his heart, he knew tonight was special.

Ever since she'd lost control and poured out her sad story to him, he'd found himself praying for her at the oddest times. At some point, his prayers had changed. Rather than only wanting to provide comfort and stability to her, he had started to pray that she would respond to him on more than a mentor level, that she would see him as a friend, then as more than just a friend, as the soul mate to share his hopes and dreams and his future. He wanted so much to pour his heart out to her, to shower her with words of love and devotion, but he doubted she was ready to hear them.

He ran his hands up her back, then released her. "I think it's time for me to take you home."

More than ever before, Jed impressed Jillian with his manners, both when he escorted her back to his truck, and when they arrived at her house. He appeared at the door of the truck, extending his hand to help her out before she even realized he was there. He'd been strangely silent on the drive home, but more than silent, what little he did say was ominously serious.

Although unsure of whether or not to invite him in, she didn't want the evening to end, so Jillian invited Jed in for a cup of tea. He graciously accepted, without commenting on how much he hated her favorite blend. The omission worried her.

As she poured the water, she peeked over her shoulder at him. His size dwarfed her small kitchen. She compared his appearance today to the last time he had been in her kitchen. On his way home from work that night, he hadn't looked like this. In contrast to his almost elegant attire tonight, his clothes then were worn, torn, and dirty. But it wasn't his garments that made the difference; it was something else, something she couldn't put her finger on.

"Relax, Jed, you're making me nervous," she quipped, trying

to sound light. She wished she could figure out what it was.

Jed leaned back in the chair, raising his arms, linking his fingers behind his head. He rested his feet on one of the chairs, crossed his ankles, and grinned. "Better?"

Jillian stared. Even the silly pose could not undermine his size and attractiveness. His dimples and white smile nearly made her heart stop. The usual lock of hair dangled rakishly onto his forehead, magnifying his good looks. "You have big feet," she stammered.

"What?" His grin dropped, he wiggled his toes, then smiled again. "At least you didn't say I have a hole in my socks."

Jillian waited for the kettle to boil, then poured water into the teapot to steep, and after a few minutes, poured the tea into two cups. The entire time, Jed said nothing, a sure indication that something was up. Slowly, she raised her teacup, hoping she could control the shaking of her hands as she gently sipped her tea. Jed straightened in the chair, following her lead.

On his first cautious sip, he grimaced, squeezed his eyes shut, and shook his head. "Yuck! This is that boiled straw again!" He opened his eyes and set the teacup on the table. "First, you make fun of me; now, you're trying to poison me."

"I beg your pardon?" Jillian gently lowered her cup to the saucer. His sour expression did indeed indicate he seriously thought he was being poisoned.

Jed closed his eyes and shook his head again. The one stray lock of unruly hair bounced with his movement. "This is the same putrid concoction you gave me before."

She couldn't help but smile. The old Jed was back.

As if trying to save face, he took another cautious sip, then again grimaced in distaste. "This brew rates up there with 'Pop Goes the Weasel.' Just so you appreciate me, I'll let you know, I'm only drinking this to be polite."

Appreciate him? Jillian appreciated him in ways she dared not admit. To distract herself, she took another sip of her tea. "For your information, it's good for you. It's a special blend, a selection meant to be enjoyed, an herbal mixture meant to aid relaxation. And don't tell me that only your mother can tell you what's good for you. I'm your teacher, and don't you ever forget it."

"Oh, so you're not trying to poison me, you're trying to put me to sleep." His eyes twinkled as he spoke.

"If you do go to sleep, at least I'll know it's the tea, and not that I'm boring you," she retorted, unable to suppress a grin.

Jed lowered his cup to the table, then reached across to cover both her hands with one of his. His large hand dwarfed hers completely. "You'll never bore me, Jillian."

Unable to respond, she yanked her hands out from under his, but in doing so, her elbow caught the edge of her teacup. The cup rattled against the saucer, then tipped, spilling the tea, sending a large puddle flowing over the tabletop. Jed jumped to his feet a split second before a waterfall of hot tea cascaded onto his chair, then dribbled onto the floor.

Jillian raised both hands to her lips. "Ooh, Jed, I'm so sorry!" She tried to stand, but Jed stopped her by resting one hand on her shoulder, preventing her from moving.

"Missed me by a mile. You stay there, I'm already up. I'll get it, before this wonderful substance strips the finish off the table."

Using her dishcloth, Jed carefully wiped up every drop, rinsed the cloth, and hung it over the faucet. He pulled down a section of paper towel, and dutifully wiped the chair and floor. "Done," he stated simply, wiping his hands on the towel.

Jillian's face flamed. Not only had she been so clumsy and spilled her tea, but she sat and watched while her guest cleaned up after her.

"Want me to pour you some more?" He picked up the teapot and sloshed it around. "There's still some in here. You didn't have a tea cozy on it, but it's probably still warm enough." He rested his hand on the outside of the teapot, feeling its warmth, then nodded. "I think I can sacrifice not having a second cup if you want it." He grinned and started pouring it without waiting for her to reply.

Sitting in the chair, Jillian's throat constricted as she watched him carefully pour the tea. She didn't know how to handle her time with Jed. He spent time with her because he enjoyed her company, and he sincerely didn't want anything she wasn't willing to give. Totally undemanding, he was fun to be with, but yet he had a serious side, both dependable and respectable. His faith in God was solid and secure, and he lived his life to honor God to the best of his ability. Although in an unconventional way, he was an invaluable support to his family, committing himself to the long term. He could be trusted. Unconditionally.

Slowly and innocently, he had worked his way into her heart. "Thank you," she choked out in a whisper. Hopefully, he couldn't hear the strain in her voice.

He rinsed out the teapot and set it upside down in the drain board. Jillian didn't want the tea, but she forced herself to drink it. Jed resumed his position in the now-dry chair, pushed his cup to the center of the table, and watched her as she sipped in silence.

"You know, I never realized how late it was. I guess I'm used to being up in the middle of the night, working the hours I do." He stood, pushing the chair in. "I should be going."

"Yes, it is late." Despite the lateness of the hour, and the supposed soothing effect of the tea, the last thing Jillian felt like was sleeping.

She walked him to the door. He stepped into his shoes,

then turned. "Good night, Jillian."

She stood beside the door, hypnotized, unable to look away. Jed turned to stand close to her, the sparkle in his eyes fading along with his smile.

Very slowly, his arms surrounded her. "I want to kiss you good night, Jillian." She noticed it wasn't a question, and if it had been, she couldn't have denied him. One hand gently drifted up her arm, brushed her throat, then cupped her chin as his eyes closed. Her eyes fluttered shut just as his lips descended on hers. Delicately, he kissed her, gently and tenderly. She was lost. He pulled away long enough to whisper gently against her lips, "I love you, Jillian."

Somewhere in the background, she heard her own voice answer back, "I love you too, Jed." She started to kiss him back when she realized what had just happened. She couldn't love him, and he couldn't love her. Panic gripped her. Not Jed. She valued his friendship and his steady companionship too much to venture past what had already been established, past the point of no return. Jed had the capacity to do more damage than anyone she'd ever known.

Jillian slid her hands to his chest and pushed. "We both have to get up for church in the morning."

Jed stiffened, then separated, but instead of fully backing away, he held both her hands between them with both of his. "Jillian?"

"I think you'd better leave." She needed time to think, and to ask for help, and in order to do that, she had to be alone with God.

His confused expression was almost her undoing. "Maybe we should talk."

Jillian shook her head. "I don't think so. Not today. Not now." She clamped her lips together before she started to babble.

Still holding both her hands with one of his larger ones, Jed gently brushed the hair off her temple, then ran two fingers down her cheek, resting them under her chin. "Will I see you tomorrow?"

Her heart pounded so hard, she thought he could surely see it. All the heat drained out of her until she shivered. "I don't think so," she squeaked.

"I see." He nodded, dropped his hands, then left.

Jillian stood in the open doorway, watching the taillights of his truck disappear into the night. The cool air against her face helped quell the sudden rush of despair as he disappeared around the corner. She'd sent him away.

She rushed inside and slammed the door shut, leaned against it, and gulped for air. What had she done? Burying her face in her hands, Jillian did the only thing she could. She talked to her Best Friend.

Dear Jesus, help me. Things are going too fast. I don't know what I should do. I can't handle this alone. As You do every time I ask, please guide me, show me what is in Jed's heart, and if it is in Your plans, if it is in Your will, tell me what to do.

Then Jillian picked up her Bible, sat on the couch, and read 1 Corinthians 13:4–7 a dozen times. Could she ever achieve those high standards for love?

twelve

Jillian walked into the sanctuary in silence, ignoring the sociable chatter around her. Sitting quietly in the pew, she tucked her purse beneath her, staring forward. As she waited for the service to begin, her head swam with conflicting images. Graham, declaring his love, demanding and expecting physical proof of hers, followed by the threat of violence if she denied what he claimed as his right. Jed and his soft words, his unspoken friendship and tenderness, demanding nothing, then holding her close when she fell to pieces and cried in his arms. She had needed him, and he'd been there for her.

No one had ever been there for her before. No one but Jesus. On the other hand, people freely called her when they needed something. At the university, she'd tutored many other aspiring music students. She'd volunteered whenever she was asked for church-related activities. Even as a child, her father loved to show off his cute little budding talent on the piano, then once the crowds were gone, off to the nanny she went. No one wanted her for what she was—simply Jillian Jefferson.

Graham, whom she had thought was a fine upstanding Christian man, let her down when he should have been different. But Jed was different from Graham. In her mind, she knew it, but in her heart, she struggled to let go of her fear. If she trusted Jed, would he be the next to disappoint her? If so, she wouldn't survive. Not again, and not from him.

Jillian closed her eyes to pray, but before she gathered her thoughts, a familiar deep voice beside her nearly caused her heart to stop. "Hi, Jillian. Mind if I sit here?"

"Jed!" A few heads turned at the volume of her squeaky voice. She lowered her pitch a few octaves. "Jed," she whispered. "What are you doing here?"

Standing tall beside her, he looked down, then lowered himself to sit in the pew beside her. "It's Sunday. I'm attending church." He slid in close beside her.

Last night, she'd opened her heart and soul to God, talking to Him at length about Jed. She'd done a lot of Bible reading and a lot of praying, and she could feel God telling her to listen to Jed, to open her heart, put all her past hurts aside, and allow herself to love him as he surely loved her. Surely that couldn't be so hard.

She started to fold her hands in her lap, but Jed grasped her left hand to hold it with his right. "I missed you."

Her throat tightened, and her heart pounded. "You just saw me last night," she whispered.

He chuckled gently, then rubbed her hand with his other one, being careful not to let go. "That was nine hours ago."

She gulped, her throat tight, almost totally constricted. "Oh, that long?"

"That's too long. We should be going to church together."

"You should be in church with your family."

"We could be family."

She turned to face him, but he was staring down at their joined hands, absently toying with her fingers. She wanted to yank her hand away, but she couldn't. Family? What did he mean by that? The only way they could be family was if they got—

The service started, drawing Jillian's attention forward. Throughout the worship songs, every time they stood, then sat, he didn't release her hand. Throughout the sermon, his grip remained gentle, but firm. During the prayer time, he squeezed her hand a number of times, as if she needed a reminder of his presence. When they stood for the closing hymn, Jed released her hand, but Jillian missed her pitch on the high note when he slipped his arm around her waist.

As soon as the pastor closed the service, with the last strums from the guitar softly accompanying his words, Jed turned to her. Again he held both her hands, then ran his fingers over her wrists. "Jillian, I need to talk to you. Alone. I wonder if—"

"Jillian! Good to see you! And who's your friend?"

Jillian forced a smile as she turned to face the pastor, who had just arrived beside them. "Pastor Lucas, this is Jed Davies."

She listened politely as the pastor welcomed Jed and then asked a few questions as they chatted. Jed responded politely to the questions about his church affiliation, and thanked him for the warm welcome to their small fellowship. Pastor Lucas laid his hand on Jed's shoulder, giving it a friendly squeeze as he kept talking.

A female voice interrupted their conversation. "Aren't you Dorothea and Peter's boy? I heard you've moved in with your sister, Elizabeth, isn't it?" All three heads turned to see the woman who was approaching, speaking as she walked.

Jed glanced back and forth between Pastor Lucas to Jillian, then back to the woman. "Yes, that's right. But I'm sorry, I don't remember you."

"I'm Christine Engels. I live next door to your Aunt Madge. How are your mom and dad?"

Jillian watched the light go on in Jed's eyes as he apparently remembered the woman. Jillian saw her chance for escape. She wouldn't be leaving him with strangers, so she didn't have to feel guilty about deserting him. She stepped back. "Excuse me, I'm meeting my sister for lunch, and I'm already late."

Jed gave Christine a polite smile. "If you'll excuse me, too, Christine, I'm sure I'll see you another time, okay?"

Christine nodded, and Jed accompanied Jillian to the parking lot.

On the one hand, Jillian wanted to know what Jed had to say, but on the other hand, she was almost afraid to ask. She unlocked her car door, quickly glanced at the time, then turned to face Jed. "We're alone now, Jed. What did you want to tell me?"

"Uh, I don't think this is quite the place. . ."

"I'm sorry to rush off, Jed, but Sue is already waiting for me. But I really want to hear what you wanted to tell me, especially if you made the special effort to come here, instead of going with your family this morning."

Jed grasped her hands, checked from side to side to make sure no one was watching, then fixed his eyes on her. Jillian blinked, then met his gaze.

He cleared his throat. "I didn't feel right about the way we parted last night, and I wanted to make sure you were okay."

That was all he wanted? To make sure she was okay? His concern broke down the last barrier. She couldn't speak as she stared up at him. Despite the fact that they were still standing in the church parking lot, she wished she could kiss him, just to show him how much she loved him.

She felt him give her hands a gentle squeeze, and his voice lowered so much she could barely hear him. "I love you, Jillian. Did you mean it when you said you loved me?"

Her throat tightened, but she had no doubt of her answer. "Yes, Jed, I did," she mumbled. "I just don't know what to do about it."

"Well, when a man and a woman fall in love, they start thinking of a future together. You know my plans for a teaching career. College will take a few years, so before we get into a long discussion, I'd like you to think about that, and what the future will hold for us."

Jillian felt all the color drain from her face. Us?

"You sound like you want to discuss something long term. Marriage. . ." She allowed her voice to trail off.

Jed smiled, then touched one finger to her cheek. "That's what usually happens, Jillian. Two people stand before God and declare their love, their commitment, and their trust in each other. You do trust me, don't you?"

She looked him straight in the eye, and nodded her assent. He wore his heart on his sleeve, the love for her was plain to see. His sincerity took her breath away. And it scared her.

"I've got to go, I'm already late. I'll phone you when I get back." She ducked into her car and headed for the mall.

When she got there, Jillian hurried into the restaurant as fast as her high heels would allow.

"Hi, Jillie. You're late."

"Something came up. Sorry about that. Hope you weren't waiting long."

Sue shook her head. "Not too long. So. How's the tall man in your life? Anything interesting to report?"

Jillian fumbled with her purse as she placed it on the seat beside her. "No."

Sue snorted. "No?"

Normally, she would discuss anything with Sue. This time, she simply couldn't.

Sue sipped her coffee, peeking over the rim of the cup as she spoke. "Too bad. So, he's still just a student, huh?"

"Something like that," Jillian mumbled.

Sue laid her menu down. "I can't stay too long; I have a million things to do. Geoff's mother took the kids for the afternoon, so I have to take advantage of that while I've got it."

The entire time she spent with her sister, Jillian's thoughts kept drifting back to Jed. She couldn't help but think of his closing question before she had to rush off. Did she trust him?

Since she met him, she'd progressed from simply enjoying his company to missing him when they weren't together. They'd gone from the usual amiable chitchat during lesson time to her pouring her troubles out to him, and yet he liked her anyway, and then declared his love. When they'd shared their goals, she had to admire him for his decision to make the sacrifices necessary to obtain his education for his teaching career, something she knew he'd be good at.

She knew he found her attractive, just as she found him attractive, yet he didn't push her beyond the limitations she'd set, or put aside the godly principles he held. She couldn't help but love him.

And he'd been the one to bring up long-term commitment. It was she who was holding back. Why?

Did she trust him?

The answer was yes, beyond any doubt. And she did want to marry him. And she wanted to give him the chance to ask her properly, which wasn't in the church parking lot.

Jillian smiled at the realization. Sue looked at her strangely, but didn't ask what was going on in her head, which was fine with Jillian. She could hardly wait to get home and phone Jed.

After the quickest lunch she'd ever had with her sister, Jillian rushed back to where she'd left her car. As she reached in her purse for her car keys, she touched a plastic wrapper. Jillian squeezed her eyes shut. In her rush, she'd forgotten to replenish her stock of reward stickers for her students, which was why she'd left the empty packet in her purse, to remind herself. She glanced at her watch, then to the mall across the street. If she ran in, a ten-minute delay could save her two hours tomorrow. Jillian crossed the parking lot, wishing she had worn more sensible shoes.

After she purchased her stickers, she walked quickly through the mall back to the exit. As she passed the food court in the center, a familiar head of unruly brown hair caught her attention. Her breath caught in her throat, and her mood lightened. It was Jed.

This could be her opportunity to apologize for her unenthusiastic response when he wanted to discuss their future together. Spending the time with her sister had been exactly what she needed. Although Sue was reasonably happy in her marriage, Jillian knew with the strength of God's love to support their marriage, she and Jed would form a bond that would be impossible to break, and when troubles came, together they would lean on God to help them along.

She no longer feared leaving herself vulnerable to Jed. She trusted him in every way. She felt both honored and humbled that such a man would choose her.

As she approached where Jed sat, he stood, as if ready to leave. Her feet skidded to a stop and her heart skipped a beat. He was not alone. He was with a woman.

Jillian blinked and stepped backward, partially hidden behind a large plant. Frantically, she searched for another way to make a discreet retreat, but she couldn't move without him seeing her. She was trapped.

Jed threw his head back and laughed. Jillian's face burned, not wanting to eavesdrop. She was so close that she could hear every word he said, yet he obviously didn't see her. All his concentration was focused on the woman he was with.

The woman stood, also laughing. The woman was everything Jillian was not. Tall, dark-complexioned, and model-slim, the woman exuded natural grace and confidence as she touched Jed's arm.

Jillian could hear Jed still laughing.

The woman spoke. "It's been too long since we got together, just the two of us."

Jed's laughter subsided as he wiped his eyes. "Much too long. I couldn't believe it was you; I was so surprised to see you here."

The woman replied, giggling. "I could say the same about you! All our failed plans to get together, and we bump into each other like this."

Jillian gasped. They planned to meet? How long had this been going on?

Jed stopped laughing, and patted his jacket pocket. "You wouldn't believe what I bought."

"You're full of surprises today, Jed. I have my ways; I'll get it out of you."

He shook his head and laughed. "No, you can't. I'm wise to all your tricks. You'll never pull one over on me again."

Something in Jillian's stomach went to war. So this was an old relationship. She knew Jed had a relationship that had an unhappy ending about the same time he lost his previous job. Was this her? Had they renewed their relationship, and were they now making up for lost time?

Jed picked up a few parcels, and handed them to the woman. When their hands touched, their fingers joined together between them. Jillian felt sick.

Jed's eyes sparkled, his face radiant. Jillian had never seen him so happy. The backs of her eyes burned, but she didn't dare move to wipe them.

"I'll tell you later, after I've had time to think about it some more. And in the meantime, we'd better get going and get you home before you're missed. We'll make real plans for next time." He let go of her hands, and they turned toward the exit.

The woman laughed again, then reached toward Jed's

pocket, the same one he had just patted. He covered it with one hand, then raised his other hand and wagged one finger at her. "Don't touch. Mine."

"I think I have an idea what that is. Ain't love grand!" she exclaimed, then giggled. They left, laughing about things Jillian could no longer hear, so intent on each other they fortunately didn't see her, hiding behind the large bushy plant.

As Jillian watched them exit the mall her stomach tightened. And he had asked if she trusted him. Was this why? Because she shouldn't have? If she hadn't chanced upon Jed and the other woman, would she ever have known? Or had he changed his mind?

The other woman. Jillian nearly choked. Holding her head high, she hurried back to her car, managing to hold back the flood of tears and anguish until she inserted the key in the ignition. What she had felt for Graham paled in comparison to the love she felt for Jed. She realized she hadn't loved Graham at all; she'd only thought she did because he was the first one to pay her attention.

Jed. She did love him, but for some reason, he'd changed his mind about loving her. Did he finally get fed up with her inability to get a grip on herself? Or had he been seeing both of them at the same time all along?

She drove home as fast as she could; as soon as she stepped into the front hall she burst into tears once again. The other woman's words echoed through her head. *Ain't love grand?*

No, love was not very grand at all.

ðŸ™¥

"Are you sure she didn't call while I was gone?"

Mark shook his head violently, sending his hair askew in a halo around his head. "No, Uncle Jed, she didn't call. Honest."

Jed checked his watch for the millionth time. How long did this lunch with her sister take? He'd made it home in plenty of time to catch her call, yet the phone remained silent. No messages registered on the machine, and he'd checked it at least a dozen times to be sure it worked. Jed sucked in a deep breath, picked up the phone, and dialed Jillian's number.

Jillian wiped her face on her sleeve and answered the phone with a shaking hand, hoping whoever it was wouldn't notice the tremor in her voice.

"Jillian? Hi, I've been waiting for you to call."

Her heart stopped, then started up in double-time. "Jed," she choked out. "I've been too busy."

"Are you free now? Can I come over? I'd like to talk to you."

She knew what he wanted to talk about. Either he was going to tell her he was seeing someone else and tell her good-bye, or he would pretend nothing was going on, spouting lies of love and devotion. Her emotions were still too raw to listen to either option. "No, not tonight." The less she spoke, the more chance she had of holding her composure. She bit her lip to keep it from quivering.

She heard Jed hesitate. "Tomorrow then?"

"No, not tomorrow, either."

A few seconds of silence hung on the line. "Tuesday?"

"Yes, I'll see you at your regular lesson time on Tuesday." She had managed to keep herself under control so far, but she knew she would soon lose it. Hearing his voice, all she could picture was him laughing and smiling at the other woman. Tears burned her eyes, and squeezing them shut wouldn't stop the flow.

Jed's voice lowered into a smooth husky tone, filled with concern. "Jillian, is something wrong? Talk to me."

Jillian couldn't. "I have to go." She hung up the phone as quickly as she could without slamming it into his ear, then unplugged it. Childish, perhaps, but she needed the time to sort everything through and get control of herself once more.

Tuesday would come soon enough.

৯

Jillian checked the clock again. In only a few minutes, Jed would arrive for his regular lesson. After two sleepless nights, she felt like a zombie, yet her nerves were so keyed up, she couldn't keep still. Every time she tried to plan what to say to him, she came up with a different answer. No commitment had ever been directly stated, but still she felt deceived.

Jillian closed her eyes, shook her head, then absently began picking through her pile of music books and stickers, sorting them into meaningless piles to keep herself busy. At the sound of Jed's knock, a handful of paper fluttered to the floor.

Jed walked in.

She stared past him, then sat in her chair beside the piano bench. "Please sit down, Jed," she stated formally.

"Hi, Jillian. I missed you. Did you have a good visit with your sister?"

"Yes, thank you. We should start right in, because we're working on your new book today." She leaned forward and opened the book, smoothing it open at the right page.

His hand touched her shoulder. "Jillian. . ." Jed mumbled in a choked voice, "talk to me."

She couldn't talk to him. Every version of every conversation she rehearsed flew out the window. Clearing her throat, Jillian put on her best teacher smile, ignored his plea, and recited the same lesson she'd done so many times before with so many children. When the clock on the wall indicated 2:45, she turned and smiled at him as best she could. "That's it," she said, trying to sound light.

Jed turned to her, his expression so sullen it nearly broke her heart. "Time for me to go get Betsy," he mumbled.

"Now that you're on the next level, I think we should cut the lessons back to once a week." As much as she wanted to see him, it hurt too much. "I'll see you next Tuesday."

"No, Jillian, I can't wait until next Tuesday. Can't we talk about this?"

Jillian choked. Her eyes burned, but she would rather die before she let him see her cry again. No matter what her head told her, in her heart, she still loved him, even though his heart belonged to someone else. As a Christian, supposedly someone who valued fidelity and trust, how could he be so casual about it?

Jed reached forward and grasped both her hands in his. "Can we have lunch together tomorrow?"

She yanked them back. "I don't know. You really should go get Betsy."

Jed straightened his back. "Yes, I should."

He walked to the tray, slipped his cowboy boots on, and left. Jillian sat and stared at the piano, then at Jed's scarf, taunting her from the coatrack beside the door.

thirteen

Jed exchanged greetings with the other men, at the same time throwing his lunch pail carelessly into his locker. The men laughed and joked as they sat on the bench and changed into their safety boots, ready to start another night. Today he did not join in their lighthearted banter. His mind was on other things.

After lacing his safety boots, he placed his cowboy boots in his locker and stood still. With his hands braced on the opening, he lowering his head, squeezed his eyes shut, and drew a deep breath. What had happened?

Tuning out the clatter around him while he still leaned half into his locker, Jed prayed. He prayed for guidance and for answers. Sure, he knew Jillian's hesitations to accept his love, but he could understand and accept that. Then, just when he finally started to hope she had managed to overcome her past experiences, she froze him out. The closeness he thought they'd developed was gone. Why? And, most importantly, what could he do about it?

"Wake up, Jed. Time to get moving!"

Jed opened his eyes and turned his head to see that everyone except for Dave had left the room to start their shift.

"Yeah, sure. Be right there." Jed closed his locker and walked to his workstation.

The night passed even more slowly than usual. He couldn't stop thinking of Jillian, but he came to no conclusions to explain the abrupt change in her attitude. Finally, he decided to come right out and ask her face-to-face what was wrong, or what he'd done to cause this sudden withdrawal.

When only a few minutes remained till the end of the shift, Jed heard a voice drifting down from the ceiling, calling his name. He looked up to see three members of his crew standing on the narrow catwalk, trying to adjust the fitting that held the cable to the center of the structure.

"Hey, Jed! Ya wanna come up here and help out?"

"Be right there." Jed called from the ground level. "What's up?"

"The walk feels a bit shaky—can you grab a toolbox and give us a hand?"

Jed couldn't believe his eyes. One of them had loosened the center supports in an effort to adjust it. If it was out of alignment, it was the duty of the senior man to report it to the maintenance department. Jed quickened his pace to fetch the toolbox, taking the stairs up two at a time.

One of the men started walking to him as they saw him approaching, and met him at the edge. He extended his arm to take the toolbox from Jed.

Jed handed it to him. "Are you sure you should be up here? You should leave it for maintenance. It's the end of the shift, anyway." The weight lifted from his arm as the other man took the toolbox, turned around, and started walking back to the center of the span.

Jed stood at the edge with his hands on his hips. It didn't feel right or safe. This was a job for someone who knew what he was doing.

Suddenly, with a creak of groaning metal, the catwalk swayed. All three men stumbled to the side at the same time, their weight jarring against the railing together. The toolbox flew over the side and crashed to the floor far below.

The sudden weight slamming against one side made the structure tilt further, and Jed heard a pop as the support they had been repairing came apart. A groan of fatigued metal sounded near Jed's feet. As he looked down, he saw that where the catwalk was connected to the concrete platform the metal joint had sheared. Only one bracket remained to support the catwalk, and it was bending. The structure was going to go down, and there were three men on it.

"Run!!!" he shouted at the top of his lungs. Then Jed did the only thing he could think of. He grabbed what he could of the railing, held on tight, pulled backward to brace himself against the weight, and prayed for strength. If he could hang on long enough, they could run off. The three of them would be killed from this height if the walkway came down with them on it, four stories up.

He felt the jarring of their footsteps all the way to the roots of his clenched teeth. He couldn't yell at them to run faster.

The joint gave way, leaving the entire weight in Jed's hands. He refused to let go with one man not all the way off. The weight pulled him forward off his feet and slammed his body down on the concrete floor. With the crashing impact, Jed saw stars. Between the pain in his chest and his face, his vision blurred, and he had difficulty breathing. He could taste blood and dirt from the concrete floor against his face. Jed never saw if the last man made it off or not. Everything started to go black. He tried to fight it.

The force and weight of the railing dragged him forward before it wrenched out of his hands, and the structure plummeted down and shattered, crashing to the ground below.

Jed gasped for breath, lying on his stomach, his head and arms hanging over the edge of the platform. He tried to move, but nothing would respond. He hurt so bad he couldn't focus, call for help, or even move.

Someone grabbed his ankles and dragged him away from the edge. As his arms went up above his head, the pain in his shoulder was so intense it made him nauseous. Everything started spinning. He thought his head would split in two. He threw up, and everything faded to black.

❧

Jillian woke up exhausted after a fitful sleep. Through all her tossing and turning, she had come to a decision. She simply could not teach Jed piano lessons anymore. After losing her heart to him, confiding in him, and now knowing that he loved someone else, she could no longer bear to carry on as if nothing had happened.

Worst of all, he had deceived her.

Jillian swiped tears from her eyes, unable to stop her lower lip from quivering. What was wrong with her? She was a hardworking, God-fearing woman. She tried her best to be honest and treat people fairly and to respect people's feelings.

As a stabbing reminder, Jed's scarf still hung on the coat-rack by the front door, taunting her.

As she got dressed, she decided to spare herself the drawn-out agony. Rather than have Jed come to her house, she would go to him, tell him she didn't ever want to see him again, and leave.

Jillian checked the time. She knew Jed got Mark off to school, so she chose to do it now and get it over with.

For a minute, she remained in her car after she parked it in front of the house, allowing herself to take a few deep breaths to compose herself before she saw him one last time. She still loved him. He had said he loved her. She sucked in a deep breath and closed her eyes, asking God for strength. One day she would work on forgiving him, but for now, she would tell him how he'd hurt her, and she would leave. She'd rehearsed her speech in her head a million times during the night. Now she would steel her nerve and do it.

Jillian stepped out of her car and carried the scarf over her arm to the front door. Holding it close, she could smell his spicy aftershave, another reminder of the closeness she had lost. Refusing to let herself cry, she held her head up high, determined to be strong. She would face him and tell him she was sorry she somehow disappointed him and say good-bye. She sucked in one last breath, for composure, and pressed the doorbell.

A dog barked, and a man who was not Jed came to the door, making her wonder if she had the right house.

"Miss Jefferson?" he asked hesitantly, recognizing her, even though she did not recognize him.

"Yes?" she mumbled, her mind blank.

"Looking for Jed?" It seemed she did have the right house after all.

"Yes, I am." She still couldn't think of a single thing to say.

"I'm Frank, his brother-in-law, Mark's dad. We've never met, but we've spoken to each other on the phone a few times. Please come in." He led Jillian inside, but did not smile a greeting. Barely polite, he seemed lost in thought and was barely aware of her existence.

Jillian stiffened her back and stood as tall as she was able. "Can I see Jed?" she managed to squeak out.

"He's not here—he didn't come home from work last night. I just got off the phone. There was an accident."

Jillian heart missed a beat, then pounded in her chest. An accident. Jed was hurt. Or worse, had he been killed? No! Her knees wobbled, and she felt sick.

Frank looked at her, his face rigid. "He apparently got hurt when a walkway collapsed. His actions saved the life of a man who was on it when it started to fall. They say Jed's injuries aren't life-threatening or anything, that he's not that badly hurt, but he is under sedation. I want to go see him, but I don't know what to do with Betsy. I don't know what to expect. If he's all connected to tubes and full of bandages I don't want her to see him yet, and I can't find a sitter."

Jillian gulped. Praise God, Jed was okay. Suddenly, nothing else mattered, not his deceit, not the other woman. She had to go see him. "If you don't mind, I'd like to go see him, and if you have a message, I'll be more than happy to relay it."

Frank looked at her and she looked at him. She waited while he thought of something to say. "Just tell him we're proud of him."

Tears welled up in her eyes. "Is he at General?"

"Yes, but they didn't say which room, and I was too dumb-founded to ask."

"I'll go now."

"Yes, and I've got to phone Liz. They didn't phone until early this morning to say they'd taken him to the hospital, and we were really worried. We got up to get ready for work, and it was only then we realized Jed hadn't come home. When the phone rang we knew something was wrong, because he would never stay out all night and leave us in the lurch for baby-sitting. Earlier, no one could tell us how badly he was hurt. Liz will be relieved to know it's not serious."

Jillian thought she had the tears under control, but they started up again. When it came to his family, Jed would always keep his promises and do what he said he would. Why couldn't he have been so faithful and loyal to her?

The drive to the hospital seemed to take forever. She found out which room he was in, and when she arrived at the ward, she located a nurse.

"I still don't know what happened, the extent of his injuries," Jillian croaked out in a whisper.

The nurse walked behind the desk and flipped through a file. "Hmm," she mumbled, in a businesslike tone. "You'll have to speak to the doctor on duty." She replaced the file to its slot, crossed her arms, and looked Jillian straight in the eye, as if waiting.

Jillian shuffled her feet, then turned her head back and forth to check both ways down the hall. "I don't see a doctor. Do you think you could page him or something?"

The nurse grumbled. "I know where he is. Wait here." She walked off, leaving Jillian alone by the nurses' station.

Jillian followed the nurse with her eyes, and when she was out of sight, Jillian quickly checked for anyone else around, then hastily pulled Jed's file from its slot.

The sheet containing a list of his injuries was right on top. The writing wasn't too sloppy, so she hurriedly scanned the list. Four broken ribs, a dislocated shoulder, multiple stitches to his hands, and his nose was broken.

Not taking the chance of getting caught reading any more in the file, she hastily replaced it in the nick of time as the nurse reappeared around the corner.

"I can't find the doctor, but Mr. Davies is resting. You may go in now."

That was all Jillian needed to hear. She hurriedly slipped into his room and stood beside him. His eyes were closed, and he seemed unaware of her presence.

He looked terrible. Most of his face was obscured with bandages that covered up his nose completely, and both his eyes were blackened, although she had heard that sometimes happened when noses were injured. His torso was completely wrapped because of his broken ribs, and his left arm was bound rigidly to his body. Both hands were completely bound by castlike bandages that covered his fingers like mittens.

If he were sleeping, she wouldn't wake him. Rather than speak, she reached out and smoothed that unruly lock of hair off his face.

His eyes opened a slit. "Jillian? What are you doing here?" he mumbled.

She tried to keep her voice from cracking. "I'm here to see you."

His eyes closed. "You don't want to see me. I feel like I've been run over by a truck."

Jillian bit her bottom lip. "Shhh." She stroked his hair again. "I love you, you know."

His eyes remained closed. "I love you, too," he mumbled, then dozed off, with what Jillian thought was a smile on his face.

She continued to watch him, forcing herself to push aside the vision of him with another woman. She couldn't help herself, she loved him no matter what. Perhaps there was a logical explanation, perhaps there wasn't. The most important thing, for now, was that he was going to be all right.

Jillian checked the time, then sat in the chair beside his bed. She didn't know how long he would sleep, but she couldn't stay all day because she had students coming. In order to cancel lessons, she needed more notice, since most of them came directly from school. She considered leaving a note for Jed, although she had no idea what to say.

As she was digging in her purse for a pen, his eyes opened. "Are you still here?"

Startled, she looked up. "How are you feeling?" It was a stupid question, because he really did look like he had been run over by a truck, just like he had said earlier. How did she expect him to respond?

"I'm going to have a bump on my nose," he groaned.

"What?"

"My nose. I'm going to have a bump on it."

Jillian watched Jed lying in the hospital bed, completely immobile and covered in various types of bandages and wrappings. "A bump on your nose? You're worried about a bump on your nose?"

"I liked my nose the way it was. Now it's going to have a bump on it." His eyes closed again, and he drifted back to sleep.

The sound of footsteps caused her to turn her head. A middle-aged man entered the room and came to a stop beside Jillian.

He shoved his hands in his pockets. "I'm Roy, Jed's supervisor."

"Hi. I'm Jillian." She wondered how to introduce herself. His friend? His teacher? Or something more, but what? Jillian swallowed hard and said nothing.

Roy turned his attention to Jed's still form. "How is he? The nurse said he was awake."

"He just drifted back to sleep."

Jed heard both Jillian and Roy's voices, but the sedatives and painkillers they had given him did their job. His head spun, and his eyes refused to open. He wondered if he did open his eyes, if the room would continue to spin, and he'd be sick. Instead of trying to do something he wasn't capable of doing at the moment, he listened to the conversation, dazed.

"How did this happen?" asked Jillian, her voice shaky.

Roy cleared his throat. "He tried to hold up the catwalk by himself when the structure started to collapse. It worked for the few seconds needed for the last man to run, jump off, and get dragged to safety, but Jed sure got banged up in the process. I came to tell him he made the difference."

Jed vividly recalled that split second when the last bracket gave way, the sensation of trying to stop it before it broke, and the agony as the weight sent him flying into the cement floor. He didn't know if the last man had made it off. When he woke up briefly in the ambulance, the attendants didn't know. Now he knew, and through the fog in his head, he thanked God for having made a difference.

He felt Jillian's fingers in his hair, and he tried to respond, but couldn't.

Her fingers stilled. "I don't know if you can hear me, Jed, but I have a message for you from Frank. He says they're very proud of you. And I have to get going now, because I have students coming soon, but I would think that your family will be coming tonight. I'll be back tomorrow."

He felt the cool air where her fingers had been, and the room fell silent. Jed allowed himself to fall asleep, anticipating her return, knowing everything would be all right after all.

≈

Jillian woke earlier than she had in years. She didn't think she'd ever been up before sunrise. It probably took longer to warm up the car than to walk the short distance, but this early in the morning, she couldn't bring herself to walk.

Tapping lightly on the door, she listened for a sign of movement inside the house. She was startled when sounds of barking echoed through the door, and then the door shook when the dog landed against it.

"Down, Missy!" It was Frank's voice, accompanied by scratching sounds and whining noises as the door opened. Frank pulled the dog back by the collar as he spoke.

"Hi, Jillian. We really appreciate you doing this for us. We're going to have to do something really special for Jed when he gets home. His being here has lifted such a burden off us about the baby-sitting. Since he's been living here, I think we've forgotten what a hassle it was in the morning. We haven't even given baby-sitting a second thought."

With the dog pulled away, Jillian walked in and placed her shoes neatly on the tray. "Yes, he takes his commitment very seriously, and he really loves the kids."

"And they really love him." As they walked up the stairs together, Jillian looked around. The house was quiet, so fortunately the ruckus with the dog at the door had not woken Mark and Betsy.

"I'll give you a quick tour of the house, and then we've got to be on our way. Liz will give you the routine."

Jillian followed Frank into the kitchen, where a woman who was obviously Liz was bending over into the fridge.

Liz turned at the same time as she stood. Tall, slender, dark hair. Jillian almost fainted. This was the woman Jed had been with at the mall.

fourteen

"Hi, Jillian, or should I say Miss Jefferson?" Liz held out her hand as a greeting. "I'm embarrassed to say that I've only met you once briefly, when Mark first signed up for lessons. The first thing I want you to know is how much we appreciate you doing this for us."

Jillian's mind reeled in shock as she shook Liz's hand. The other woman was his sister! How could she have been so stupid? How could she have been so untrusting? Just because Jed said he and his sister were a lot alike was no reason to assume they also looked alike.

Looking at Liz up close, now that she knew, of course, Jillian could see the family resemblance. She tried to regain her composure. "Hi, Liz, it's nice to meet you again."

"Yes—but it was supposed to be under better circumstances."

Jillian wondered what Liz meant by that comment. "You had better give me a rundown on the routine for the day so you can make it on time for work."

As Liz gave Jillian the schedule for the day, Jillian tried not to smile. Most of it she already knew from Jed, especially the afternoon schedule.

Before they left, Liz woke Betsy up and introduced her to Jillian so she would not awaken to find a stranger in the house. When Mark got up, he was delighted to have his piano teacher there to get him ready for school, although he took special care not to let Jillian see him in his pajamas.

After Mark was out the door and on his way to school, she made a pot of coffee and Betsy joined her at the kitchen table.

"Uncle Jed talks about you all the time, you know."

Jillian studied Betsy's face. She wasn't sure she wanted to hear this. "He talks about you, too."

"He does?"

Jillian gave a sigh of relief. She had managed to distract Betsy. "Yes. He says you are doing very well in kindergarten, and your teacher is very proud of you."

"You're Uncle Jed's teacher. Are you proud of him?"

Maybe this had backfired a little. Jillian tried not to let her nervousness with the little girl show. "Yes, I am."

"He thinks you're a good teacher."

"Well, I think he's a good student."

"He likes you, you know."

Great. Woman talk with a five-year-old. "Well, I like him too. Say, how would you like to help me make some cookies? I'll bet you know where your mom keeps everything, don't you?"

"Yes! I love to bake cookies. Uncle Jed tried to make cookies once. They were kind of awful. But Missy liked them. Except she barfed up the walnuts."

Jillian managed to keep a straight face. She knew Jed started supper every day, but maybe it was too much to expect that his culinary skills extended beyond that.

They took all morning to get one batch of cookies mixed and baked and the dishes done, but it was worth the mess and effort to keep Betsy busy. After a quick lunch, Jillian drove Betsy to school and then continued on her way to the hospital to visit Jed.

The entire trip, she tried to sort out what she was going to say to him. She had behaved like a jealous fool, and now she was going to have to swallow her pride and face him.

Lunch was being served as she arrived at his ward. She could hear him complaining before she walked into his room.

"How do you expect me to eat this? This isn't funny!" he griped, but she could tell he had a smile on his face without even looking. The nurses were giggling.

"The department decided to hold a raffle to see who was going to come in to help you. Proceeds go to Children's Hospital Fund." There was more giggling.

Jillian heard Jed mumble something about not being very amused, and she walked in to see for herself what was going on.

Jed looked up, causing the two nurses to turn around.

"Oh, she's here," one of them sighed. "Looks like the lunch raffle's off. Maybe suppertime." Then they both left, pushing the lunch cart out the door.

Jillian frowned and glared at Jed. "What's going on in here?" She folded her arms against her chest.

Jed had been propped up to a sitting position in the bed. He let his head drop backward. "I hate this place!" he grumbled. "Let me out of here!"

"Why?"

"With one arm strapped up like this, I can't move without someone helping me, and I can't touch or hold anything with my hands wrapped up solid. I feel like I've been mummified! I can't move, I can't eat, I can't do anything!"

Jillian tried to stifle a laugh. If this was the way he was talking to her, she could only imagine what he said to the nurses. However, she was going to have to check out this raffle.

"I can feed you. What's for lunch?" Jillian peeked under the lid of the lunch tray and laughed. Soup and a sandwich. No wonder he was complaining. And coffee, too. How would he drink that without using his hands? She couldn't imagine drinking coffee through a straw.

Jillian lifted up the sandwich so he could take a bite. He

made a wry face, but took a bite anyway.

"They barely have enough food on here to feed a pigeon. And you are not going to spoon-feed me that soup. This is so humiliating," he grumbled.

Their conversation for the balance of the afternoon mostly consisted of Jed's semi-good-natured complaining.

Jillian looked at the time. "Say 'that's it,' " she ordered.

"That's it?" he questioned.

"Yup," Jillian stated. "Time for me to go get Betsy."

"What? You?"

"Liz and Frank couldn't get a replacement for you on short notice, so I volunteered until you're up to it."

"Jillian, I don't know what to say."

"Say nothing then. Actually, they're very nice people."

"Of course they are. Frank couldn't have found a better wife than Liz. She's great. You know, we used to fight constantly when we were kids, but now, we've become the best of friends, as well as brother and sister."

Jillian's smile faded. She couldn't put it off any longer, and since he had started the topic of his sister, it forced her to say what she had been agonizing over.

"Jed, speaking of your sister, I'm afraid I have a confession to make."

"What about Liz? You two didn't have a fight, did you?"

Jillian looked down, unable to face him as she spoke. "You're probably wondering why I acted so cold to you the other day. Well, I feel so stupid about this, but I saw you and Liz together on Sunday as you were leaving the mall. From what I saw I thought you were seeing someone else, and it looked like you were exchanging words of love, and," Jillian paused and swallowed, her voice dropping to a whisper, "and I was hurt. And very jealous." She shrugged her shoulders but couldn't look up at him. "I didn't know it was your sister. I'm so sorry." Tears welled up in her eyes, and she couldn't blink them away.

"Look at me." Jed's words were soft and gentle.

Jillian couldn't face him. She swiped the tears away with her sleeve.

"We probably made quite a scene, Liz and I, carrying on at the mall, and I think I can remember what we said as we were leaving. If that's what you saw, I think I can understand why you felt that way. But you missed the best part of the conversation. We were talking about you."

Jillian blinked, but a tear escaped and ran down her cheek.

"Come here. I wish I could hold you properly, but I'll do my best."

As Jillian sat on the bed beside him, he rested his unbound arm around her as best he could.

"I love you, Jed. I'm so sorry."

"I love you, too. And don't worry about it anymore. Now, the air is clear. It's okay. Now, come here and kiss me."

Jillian stood, bent at the waist, then kissed him lightly and briefly on the mouth. "I have to go get Betsy. I'll be back tomorrow. Oh, and give me your keys so someone can pick up your truck at the plant."

"You have to get them yourself. Right there, in the drawer."

"See you tomorrow."

"Yeah, bye."

Jillian walked around the nurse who was standing near the doorway and left.

❧

Jillian arrived at the hospital the same time as the day before. However, this time she was not allowed to go into Jed's room, as the doctor was in with him, checking him over before releasing him.

She sat in a chair by the nurses' station and listened. Jed

was complaining again. First something tickled, then something pinched. Next, he refused to do something, followed by a question about why he was not allowed to do something else. Then she heard a nurse asking him to be quiet and quit moving. Jillian was glad she wasn't the one looking after him.

Finally, the nurse at the desk allowed her to enter. Jed was sitting upright in the bed with a grumpy look on his face and considerably fewer wrappings than the day before. A doctor washed his hands in the sink, and a nurse picked up the scraps of the bandages that had been removed.

"Hi, Jed," Jillian said, trying not to laugh at his dour expression. "Liz sent you some clothes. I've come to take you home."

"Yes! Freedom!" Jed shouted in triumph.

She waited in the hall for him to get dressed, but since his hands were still heavily bandaged, she helped him slip on his boots and tied the laces. "That's it," she said as she stood. "Not only that, it's time to go get Betsy."

Jed shrugged his shoulders. "What a classic line."

She led him to the parking lot, where he stopped dead in his tracks. "This is my truck! You drove my truck."

Jillian blushed. "My car is so small I didn't know how you would fit in it. I hope you don't mind."

She wasn't sure how he'd feel about her driving his truck, because some men were kind of funny about that kind of thing. Instead of being angry, though, Jed looked down at her and laughed. "You probably looked ridiculous, a little thing like you, driving a big truck like this. I'll bet you got some strange looks on the way here, didn't you?"

"Yes, as a matter of a fact, I did. I was tempted to show off, too, but I drove your precious truck with lots of TLC; I didn't do any racing with it. But I could have driven right over top of the competition." When he laughed again, Jillian knew she'd done the right thing.

"Let's go."

When Jillian drove up to the school, Jed waited inside the truck while Jillian went into the building to get Betsy. When they returned, Mark was sitting inside beside Jed. Apparently he'd noticed the huge lumbering vehicle as he was coming out of the door, and all his friends had to check it out.

On the way home, Mark and Betsy were asking Jed a million questions. When they arrived at the house, Jillian made coffee while Mark and Betsy went into their rooms to play. Once it was finished brewing, Jillian handed Jed a cup, after arguing with him over whether or not he would be able to hold it. They lounged back on the couch and Jillian turned on the television.

Suddenly, Jed's eyes widened as he stared at the time on the VCR. "Look at the time; you're late for your lessons! You'd better get going."

"No, I canceled my afternoon lessons. I wanted to stay with you until after Frank and Liz get home." She raised her hands and slowly brushed both of Jed's cheeks with her fingertips.

"Wow. Personal attention from the teacher. I could get used to this." Jed smiled and Jillian's heart melted. She leaned toward him at the same time he leaned to her, joining together for a wonderful kiss, a kiss that was sweet and made up for the waste of lost time. Briefly, they separated, their eyes drifted open, shut again, then they joined again in a warm embrace, anticipating the next kiss. A thump on the floor interrupted them.

"Gross! Uncle Jed! Miss Jefferson! That's sick!"

Jed and Jillian bolted apart. Jillian's stomach clenched. Out of the corner of her eye she saw Jed wince, suck in a deep breath, and press his arm against his ribs with the abrupt movement.

Mark stood in front of them, a large ball in his hand and Betsy at his side, both of them wide-eyed, staring at their every movement. To her dismay, Jillian had forgotten about them.

"Eeww!" Mark exclaimed, with the same disgusted look on his face as the other time he had interrupted them. "Uncle Jed, why are you letting Miss Jefferson kiss you again? You said you didn't want to marry Miss Jefferson."

Startled, Jillian backed further away. Jed's face turned red, but he didn't say a thing. She remembered when Jed brought up marriage, and at the time it had frightened her and they agreed to discuss it later. It hadn't come up again between them, but to have Mark not only mention it but say Jed had no intention of marrying her made her wonder what had been said. Why would he have said something to Mark, and most of all, what?

Betsy grabbed Mark's T-shirt and started yanking on it. "I heard Mom and Dad talking about it. Wanna know what Mom said?"

Jillian glared at Jed. All the color drained out of his face.

She jumped to her feet. She had made a mistake about his sister, but to hear from the children's mouths that Jed had said he had no intention of marrying her, with no immediate denial on his part, was more than she could take. She took a step back. "I think I had better leave."

"Jillian, wait!" Jed jumped to his feet, then tottered slightly. "Please, Jillian, wait. I have to get something, and I'll be right back. Promise me you'll wait right here." He looked at her with such a tortured expression that Jillian conceded. She hugged herself with both arms and leaned against the wall to wait for his return.

His movements were labored as he tried to hurry down the hall, then slowed as he made his way down the stairs. He returned with a small bag, and sat on the couch. He patted the seat beside him, and held out a small bag.

"Take it, Jillian, with all my love."

Jillian sat beside him, and as she took the bag from his hands, her own hands started to shake. She recognized the logo as belonging to the large jewelry store in the mall. Peeking inside, she could see a small velvet box.

"Open it." Jed's deep voice trembled.

As she picked up the box, Betsy and Mark stepped closer to see what it was. With all eyes on her, Jillian opened it. It was a small heart-shaped ring, with a small sparkling diamond set in the middle. It was delicate, and it was beautiful.

Jed's bandaged hand rested on her knee. "Jillian, I'd like to plan for the future, and I want you to be in my future. I had intended to talk about it later, and, well, now that we're together, I can't wait. Jillian, will you think about marrying me?" he said in a low husky voice. "This wasn't the way I intended to ask you something so important, but it couldn't be helped. I can't let you walk away from me again."

Jillian's vision blurred as she raised her head to look into his eyes.

"You bought this at the mall," she choked on the words, "the day I saw you there with your sister."

"That's right. It's just a little promise ring, because it's going to be a long time before I finish my education. If you'll wait for me, I wanted to give you this ring as a promise. But if you say yes now, we can go together so you can pick your own engagement ring."

Jillian swallowed, hard. "Yes, of course I'll marry you. But your education comes first, before an engagement ring."

One side of his mouth tipped up in a lopsided smile. "It's taken care of. I was going to take out a student loan, but as it turns out, yesterday I had another visitor in the hospital. An old friend stopped by and it seems she saw the error of her ways, turned her life over to Jesus, and paid back a lot of money she owed me. So, don't you worry about that."

Jillian's heart pounded. God had carried her through her trials and hurts, and helped her to rise above them. Now she could love Jed as he deserved to be loved. God had given her the best gift of all, and she didn't have to do anything to receive it. She'd received the gift of love, both through the salvation of Jesus Christ, and the commitment of a wonderful, God-fearing man. Her voice dropped to a choked whisper. "I love you so much, Jed."

"I love you, too, Jillian."

At the same moment, they both turned their heads to see Mark and Betsy, who were staring at them with their mouths hanging open, still watching, and listening to every word.

"Okay you two, beat it, or you're going to have to watch Uncle Jed kiss Miss Jefferson."

Mark ran away first. "Yuck! No! Anything but that!" he screamed as he ran. Betsy shrieked, following his example, and ran after him.

Then Uncle Jed kissed Miss Jefferson like she had never been kissed before.

A Letter To Our Readers

Dear Reader:

In order that we might better contribute to your reading enjoyment, we would appreciate your taking a few minutes to respond to the following questions. We welcome your comments and read each form and letter we receive. When completed, please return to the following:

Rebecca Germany, Fiction Editor
Heartsong Presents
PO Box 719
Uhrichsville, Ohio 44683

1. Did you enjoy reading *Piano Lessons?*
   ❏ Very much. I would like to see more books
   by this author!
   ❏ Moderately
   I would have enjoyed it more if _____

   _____

   _____

2. Are you a member of **Heartsong Presents**? Yes ❏ No ❏
   If no, where did you purchase this book? _____

   _____

3. How would you rate, on a scale from 1 (poor) to 5 (superior), the cover design? _____

4. On a scale from 1 (poor) to 10 (superior), please rate the following elements.

   _____ Heroine   _____ Plot

   _____ Hero   _____ Inspirational theme

   _____ Setting   _____ Secondary characters

5. These characters were special because _____

_____

_____

6. How has this book inspired your life? _____

_____

_____

7. What settings would you like to see covered in future
   Heartsong Presents books? _____

_____

_____

8. What are some inspirational themes you would like to see
   treated in future books? _____

_____

_____

9. Would you be interested in reading other **Heartsong
   Presents** titles?   Yes ☐   No ☐

10. Please check your age range:
    ☐ Under 18   ☐ 18-24   ☐ 25-34
    ☐ 35-45   ☐ 46-55   ☐ Over 55

11. How many hours per week do you read? _____

Name _____

Occupation _____

Address _____

City _____ State _____ Zip _____

How can love flourish in such a frozen frontier?

*S*urviving the rugged frontier of Alaska is a daunting task. But even in that hostile wilderness, God allows the tender flower of love to bloom. Follow the adventures and romances of Julie, Beth, and Rita, women of different generations who share a common home—*Alaska*. Their stories are told by best-selling author Tracie Peterson in three novels and one bonus novella.

Stories that span the range of human emotion: loneliness, anger, fear, joy, and love. Stories that demonstrate God's leading in human lives. The stories of *Alaska*.

400 pages, Paperbound, 5 ³⁄₁₆" x 8"

Please send me _____ copies of *Alaska*. I am enclosing $4.97 each.
(Please add $1.00 to cover postage and handling per order. OH add 6% tax.)
Send check or money order, no cash or C.O.D.s please.

Name_____

Address _____

City, State, Zip _____

To place a credit card order, call 1-800-847-8270.
Send to: Heartsong Presents Reader Service
PO Box 719, Uhrichsville, OH 44683

·····Hearts♥ng·····

Any 12
Heartsong
Presents titles
for only
$26.95 **

CONTEMPORARY
ROMANCE IS CHEAPER
BY THE DOZEN!

**Buy any assortment of twelve
Heartsong Presents titles and
save 25% off of the already
discounted price of $2.95 each!**

**plus $1.00 shipping and handling per order and
sales tax where applicable.

HEARTSONG PRESENTS *TITLES AVAILABLE NOW:*

__HP149 LLAMA LAND, *VeraLee Wiggins*

__HP177 NEPALI NOON, *Susannah Hayden*

__HP178 EAGLES FOR ANNA, *Cathrine Runyon*

__HP181 RETREAT TO LOVE, *Nancy N. Rue*

__HP182 A WING AND A PRAYER, *Tracie J. Peterson*

__HP185 ABIDE WITH ME, *Una McManus*

__HP186 WINGS LIKE EAGLES, *Tracie J. Peterson*

__HP189 A KINDLED SPARK, *Colleen L. Reece*

__HP190 A MATTER OF FAITH, *Nina Coombs Pykare*

__HP193 COMPASSIONATE LOVE, *Ann Bell*

__HP194 WAIT FOR THE MORNING, *Kjersti Hoff Baez*

__HP197 EAGLE PILOT, *Jill Stengl*

__HP198 WATERCOLOR CASTLES, *Ranee McCollum*

__HP201 A WHOLE NEW WORLD, *Yvonne Lehman*

__HP202 SEARCH FOR TODAY, *Mary Hawkins*

__HP205 A QUESTION OF BALANCE, *Veda Boyd Jones*

__HP206 POLITICALLY CORRECT, *Kay Cornelius*

__HP209 SOFT BEATS MY HEART, *Aleesha Carter*

__HP210 THE FRUIT OF HER HANDS, *Jane Orcutt*

__HP213 PICTURE OF LOVE, *Tamela Hancock Murray*

__HP214 TOMORROW'S RAINBOW, *VeraLee Wiggins*

__HP217 ODYSSEY OF LOVE, *Melanie Panagiotopoulos*

__HP218 HAWAIIAN HEARTBEAT, *Yvonne Lehman*

__HP221 THIEF OF MY HEART, *Catherine Bach*

__HP222 FINALLY, LOVE, *Jill Stengl*

__HP225 A ROSE IS A ROSE, *Ruth Richert Jones*

__HP226 WINGS OF THE DAWN, *Tracie J. Peterson*

__HP229 TREASURE OF THE KEYS, *Stephen A. Papuchis*

__HP230 AFTERGLOW, *Irene B. Brand*

__HP233 FAITH CAME LATE, *Freda Chrisman*

__HP234 GLOWING EMBERS, *Colleen L. Reece*

__HP237 THE NEIGHBOR, *Debra Whitesmith*

__HP238 ANNIE'S SONG, *Andrea Boeshaar*

__HP241 DESTINY, ARIZONA, *Marty Crisp*

__HP242 FAR ABOVE RUBIES, *Becky Melby and Cathy Wienke*

__HP245 CROSSROADS, *Tracie Peterson and Jennifer Peterson*

__HP246 BRIANNA'S PARDON, *Gloria Clover*

(If ordering from this page, please remember to include it with the order form.)

······· Presents ·······

Great Inspirational Romance at a Great Price!

Heartsong Presents books are inspirational romances in contemporary and historical settings, designed to give you an enjoyable, spirit-lifting reading experience. You can choose wonderfully written titles from some of today's best authors like Veda Boyd Jones, Yvonne Lehman, Tracie Peterson, Debra White Smith, and many others.

When ordering quantities less than twelve, above titles are $2.95 each.
Not all titles may be available at time of order.

SEND TO: **Heartsong Presents** Reader's Service
P.O. Box 719, Uhrichsville, Ohio 44683

Please send me the items checked above. I am enclosing $_____
(please add $1.00 to cover postage per order. OH add 6.25% tax. NJ add 6%.). Send check or money order, no cash or C.O.D.s, please.
To place a credit card order, call 1-800-847-8270.

NAME_____

ADDRESS _____

CITY/STATE_____ ZIP _____

HPS 13-98

Hearts♥ng Presents
Love Stories Are Rated G!

That's for godly, gratifying, and of course, great! If you love a thrilling love story, but don't appreciate the sordidness of some popular paperback romances, **Heartsong Presents** is for you. In fact, **Heartsong Presents** is the *only inspirational romance book club*, the only one featuring love stories where Christian faith is the primary ingredient in a marriage relationship.

Sign up today to receive your first set of four, never before published Christian romances. Send no money now; you will receive a bill with the first shipment. You may cancel at any time without obligation, and if you aren't completely satisfied with any selection, you may return the books for an immediate refund!

Imagine. . .four new romances every four weeks—two historical, two contemporary—with men and women like you who long to meet the one God has chosen as the love of their lives. . .all for the low price of $9.97 postpaid.

To join, simply complete the coupon below and mail to the address provided. **Heartsong Presents** romances are rated G for another reason: They'll arrive *Godspeed!*

YES! Sign me up for Hearts♥ng!

NEW MEMBERSHIPS WILL BE SHIPPED IMMEDIATELY!
Send no money now. We'll bill you only $9.97 post-paid with your first shipment of four books. Or for faster action, call toll free 1-800-847-8270.

NAME _____

ADDRESS _____

CITY _____ STATE _____ ZIP _____

MAIL TO: HEARTSONG PRESENTS, P.O. Box 719, Uhrichsville, Ohio 44683

YES10-96